Sibyl Sue Blue

Rosel George Brown

Journey Press
journeypress.com

Vista, California
Journey Press

Journey Press
P.O. Box 1932
Vista, CA 92085

CREDITS
Cover design: Sabrina Watts at Enchanted Ink Studio

First Printing July 2021

ISBN: 978-1-951320-08-9

Published in the United States of America

JourneyPress.com

To Burlie

Introduction

Sibyl Sue Blue was not what I expected.

Set in the futuristic year of 1990, Rosel George Brown's *Sibyl Sue Blue* takes place in a world both like and unlike 1966 — the year it was released. Sibyl is a tenacious and smart detective working for the city's homicide department. When a series of bizarre 'suicides' start plaguing the city's youth, she's called in to investigate. As she follows the clues, she's drawn into increasingly strange events, from trying alien drugs to being invited to join a spacefaring millionaire on an off-world jaunt.

Sounds like fun, right? And somehow, I went into it looking for the "...froth and fun and furious action," promised by Judith Merril's review, without ever considering the rest of the quote:

> And the damnedest part of it is that under all the froth and fun and furious action, there is more acute comment on contemporary society than you are likely to find in any half dozen deadly serious social novels.

That's not to say that *Sibyl Sue Blue* is dry, boring, or preachy. In fact, it's the exact opposite of these things. But, as Merril promised, beneath the wild ride exists a sharp yet understated criticism of both modern racial tensions and treatment of women in science fiction.

Let's take racial tensions, for example. When I say that SSB offers subtle commentary on race relations, I'm not talking about the obvious parallels between the story's alien Centaurians and modern day people of color. That analogy is obvious to anyone with half a brain: places where the 'aliens' have moved in have become ghettos, they smoke strange cigarettes, and they are generally distrusted by the human population — but if you're a cop, you don't dare say so.

I'll admit, it threw me for a loop at first. What was with this heavy-handed analogy? It wasn't until I read further into the story that I got it. The subtlety comes into play in Sibyl's interactions with Centaurians, as well as Brown's portrayal of them. Throughout the story Sibyl treats Centaurians the same way she treats humans. Though she warns her colleague not to get caught saying he doesn't like Centaurians, never once does Sibyl herself express dislike or distrust of a Centaurian simply because they are Centaurian. In fact, though the story opens with her being attacked by a Centaurian, her sharp mind is already searching for the *reason* behind his actions.

Then, too, Brown's portrayals of Centaurians are as variegated as her portrayals of humans. They're not saints, but they're no worse than anyone else, and better than many. And like humans, they can be coerced, manipulated, and used by people or entities more powerful than themselves.

There's a certain cynicism coloring everything. The good-hearted and earnest "Jimmy" says things like, "Gee, it's a shame about Centaurian prejudice," and sounds hopelessly naive. Yet only a couple of chapters later, Sibyl doesn't hesitate to invite her Centaurian friend, contact, and occasional lover over for some info and an intimate pick-me-up. The contrast between Sibyl's attitude and Jimmy's is telling. It's not enough to criticize prejudice, Sibyl (and Brown) seems to be saying. You need to walk the walk, not just talk the talk. And Sibyl walks it—boy, does she!

Speaking of walking the walk, another thing that startled me, at least until I got what Brown was doing, was the story's 'romantic' subplot.

At the time *Sibyl Sue Blue* came out, multiple science fiction magazines and occasional science fiction novels, TV shows, and movies were released each month in the USA and the UK. In a good month, maybe ten percent of the fifty or sixty stories published were penned by women. In a bad month, *none* of the stories were written by a woman. The average usually fell somewhere in-between.

Perhaps it isn't a surprise, then, that so few protagonists of contemporaneous science fiction tales were women. Whether written by men or women, whether they were complex and interesting or shallow and flat, main characters were overwhelmingly white men. When women did show up, they were often relegated to the role of helpmate, something in need of rescuing, or the prize the man won after overcoming his trials—sometimes all three!

Obviously, there are plenty of exceptions, but in terms of trends, if a beautiful woman was introduced into a story (or a TV show, or a movie) in the first act, chances were she would fall in love with the male lead by the end. This was true regardless of how unappealing, uninteresting, or unlikeable the man was.

This cliché is another that *Sibyl Sue Blue* turns on its head. What is it like to *be* the woman who seemingly inexplicably falls for a rich, handsome, clever, yet completely terrible man? What happens when a woman who is herself independent, interesting, and already has her own life suddenly gets caught up in the implacable tide of the plot?

Traditionally, the woman would marry the man after he solved the case and the two would live 'happily' ever after. But as I found when I kept reading, if the woman is someone like Sibyl Sue Blue, nothing will turn out the way you expect!

Sibyl is fascinating. She's small but powerful, repeatedly shown as able to hold her own in a fight, even against men who are bigger than she. Yet she's also unapologetically feminine. She enjoys wearing nice dresses, applying makeup, and accessorizing. Far from being stoic, when something terrifying and grotesque happens, she screams. When she's overwhelmed, she cries.

And then she gets up and keeps going. Like so many women throughout history, when faced with circumstances far beyond her control, when she's sick and exhausted and frightened, she keeps pushing forward.

Sibyl Sue Blue has silver stripes in her hair and a daughter in high school. She's strong and vulnerable and smart. She enjoys a startling amount of sexual freedom, unhesitatingly inviting handsome men to her bed as a matter of course. Above all, she is *herself*—not an easily categorized and dismissed 'helpmate', 'damsel in distress', or 'prize'. She's human and messy and makes mistakes and is sometimes clever. She's as complex and interesting as the best of the male leads, and maybe even more than any of them.

Because I've read the stories of a lot of white men, but I've never met a character like Sibyl Sue Blue.

—Janice Marcus

CHAPTER I

Sibyl Sue Blue didn't stop to think. She slung her handbag like a sledge and knocked the gun out of his hand. She kneed him where it hurt the most and then rabbit punched him. It's the same place for Centaurians as it is for humans.

There was a shrill scream of brakes and a cop in well-fitting regulation browns got out and cupped his heavy hand on Sibyl's shoulder.

"O.K., lady," he said. "I don't like 'em either. But it's against the law to beat 'em up... Gee, what a little bitty girl you are!"

Sibyl flipped back her wig and spit out her cheekpieces. "Stanley, you idiot! Don't you recognize me?"

"Sergeant Blue! Excuse me. How was I to know? Here you were acting like a bouncer and looking like my little sister. Gee. I never seen you in disguise before. You're a credit to the force."

Sibyl brushed herself off, glanced down the empty street of Old Town and lit a cigar. "Thank you, Stanley. Let the Centaurian get himself up and forget you saw this. It's a new development, Centaurians attacking me, and I think it ties in with the benzale murders. But keep your mouth *closed*, honey. Every time a Centaurian on Terra gets bruised the State Department is on our necks. And a cop should *never* say he doesn't like Centaurians."

Stanley sighed and looked sheepish. He took off his hat and scratched his crinkly hair. "I know. But look what a slum they've made out of Old Town. When I was a child Page Grant hadn't discovered Centaurus and this was a pretty neighborhood. In ten years they've brought all the vices of New York City to Hammond."

"Page Grant's dead and Hammond is a spaceport and you can't turn back the clock." Sibyl toed out the rest of her fresh cigar regret-

1

fully. "I don't have time to point out all the virtues of Centaurians. Buy me a gin and 'gin some time and we can chat more cosily."

"Gee, Sergeant, I'm a married man."

"Well, bring your wife."

Sibyl glanced at her watch. This was going to make her ten minutes late. She hurried on down the dirty, picturesque alleys of Old Town, stepped onto the moving sidewalk at the Throughway and elbowed a square-faced, middle-aged woman who was hogging the middle.

The woman sniffed. "No manners, these young people." Sibyl grinned broadly and then said, "I'm sorry, ma'am. I'm going to meet my boy friend."

She gave the woman a gentle kick in the shins as she hopped over the Moderator at Eighth and Avenue A, spent one second fluffing out her bright brown wig and adjusting the expression on her face, and then trotted on her little high heels into the jumble of plastic cubes with the sign that said "Korner Klub."

A big, black-haired boy whose pimples were almost finished treatment looked up at her from his seat at the counter, and wriggled into smiles all over.

"Gee, baby, you're late," he said. "I was worried, you being in Old Town and all."

"Strawberry soda," Sibyl ordered, and let him punch for it. She turned her baby blue eyes on him. "A man tried to pick me up, Jimmy. An old man about thirty-five." She shivered.

Jimmy tensed. "I wished I would of been there. I'd of shown him what for. What did you do?"

"Well, I didn't know what to do. I ran." Sibyl bent down to mesh the splitting ankle seam on her stocking, and at the edge of the one-way cubicle in the comer she saw an elbow that looked familiar. A greenish Centaurian elbow. "But that's why I'm late. I got lost running and I had to find the Uptown Throughway."

Jimmy put a protective arm around her. "You shun't of took a project like that," he said. "How the houses are in Old Town."

"Well, I was interested. My mother says it used to be a good neighborhood even ten years ago. Before so many Centaurians moved in. You know." Did that greenish Centaurian just happen to be here or

2

was he after Sibyl? Benzale pushers didn't usually hang around the Korner Klub.

"Yeah," Jimmy said. "But that was 1980 and this is 1990. Gee, it's a shame about Centaurian prejudice. It isn't them. It's the humans. You'll see at the C meeting."

"Excuse me," Sibyl said, taking a quick gulp of her soda and slotting in a quarter before Jimmy could take the treat. "I have to go rouge my knees. I look a mess from all that running."

She heel-clicked across the fake marble and whisked out of sight into the one-way cubicle.

The Centaurian was just getting his needle gun out when Sibyl pulled off one of her shoes and made a nice dent the size of a stiletto heel in his temple.

Through the one-way glass of the cubicle Sibyl saw Jimmy absently fingering the bowl around his chocolate sundae and glancing at the Ladies'. As soon as he glanced outside to watch the new Tireless Triumph go by, she slipped out of the cubicle and into the Ladies'.

Sibyl straightened her stockings above the calf, got out her rouge stick and rouged her knees. Then she took a little jar of skin cream, spread it around her eyes and mouth and carefully ironed out tiny wrinkles with her finger.

The Centaurian would be out another ten minutes. If he wasn't dead, of course.

Sibyl went back to the counter, gave Jimmy a smile that made the sweat pop out on his forehead, drank up her strawberry soda in one gulp and slid off the stool.

"Bye-bye, Jimmy," she said, hopping gracefully onto the Middle Throughway as Jimmy watched her from the door. "Wait for me outside at the Centaurian meeting tonight." She needed Jimmy to get her in.

Sibyl glanced at her watch. Almost four o'clock. She went on to the apartment, pressed her contact key against the door and went in.

"Hi, Mom," Missy said. "Working today?"

"As usual," Sibyl answered with a sigh. She couldn't reach over and muss Missy's hair any more. It might ruin a five-dollar set. "What've you got on for this big Saturday night?"

"A game against Beman High. Party afterwards, strictly low dog.

Want me out?"

"Probably. It's sheer luck you're a nice girl, Missy, after the way I've raised you."

"Heredity," Missy said, and kissed her mother fondly. "Anyway, what's wrong with the way you've raised me?"

Sibyl sighed and sat down, feeling suddenly tired. "Well, it's kind of hard to be a policewoman and a mother at the same time. It was different when we had your father. When you were a baby Kenneth worked at home a lot. He just went to the university to teach his biochemistry classes, and dropped by Centaurus Research for his fat consulting fee. But just about the time he disappeared on Radix, I started getting outside assignments that meant more pay but irregular hours."

Missy stuffed her gym clothes into her blue bag. "You couldn't stand an office job, Mama. I know that. And I wouldn't want it any different. A lot of kids go crazy with their mother home every evening by four or five. Not that I don't have fun with you, but..."

"O.K.," Sibyl said with a grin. "You've convinced me."

Missy dragged a purple lipstick across her mouth without bothering with a mirror, grabbed her blue bag and started out of the door.

Sibyl sighed after her beautiful, long brunette daughter. If only Kenneth had lived to see her at sixteen. Kenneth... well, it would all have been different. Or would it? You never knew, about yourself.

Sibyl pinched out her blue contact lenses and blinked her bright green eyes. Then she pulled off her wig. Her hair was startling. It was black-and-gray-striped and it grew that way naturally. She relaxed her face and took out the cheekpieces. Now she looked nearer forty. But it wasn't a bad forty, not bad at all and Sibyl knew it. And used it. It was part of her job.

She spent fifteen minutes relaxing utterly in a cottony Float Foam bath, not allowing herself to think about plain Centaurians or greenish Centaurians or benzale murders. She sipped lazily at a gin and 'gin and lit a delicate golden cigar.

Me, she thought, enjoying the blue bubbles of the Float Foam that held her suspended in a fizzy warmth. I'll think about Me. She watched the soft, gray cigar smoke disperse against the sky-blue tiles of her bath.

4

I'm lucky. I've got a beautiful daughter and a good figure no matter how much I eat, and naturally curly hair...

The only thing I don't have is a man. At the moment.

Now who haven't I seen in a long time? she thought. There was Jackson Small with the brokerage firm. But he had that irritating way of looking so neat Sibyl always felt she had to check over herself every few minutes to be sure her stockings were meshed and her hair in place... No, Jackson was nice but... well, now there was Scaley Moe — Llanr. Scaley Moe was just the opposite. Like most Centaurians...

Llanr! Sibyl sat up and smashed out her cigar in the disposall. Llanr would be at Joe's Bar about now for his evening toddy. It had been too long since she'd seen him. If anybody knew why green Centaurians couldn't look at Sibyl Sue Blue without wanting to attack her, he would.

Sibyl spent a moment in the drier, turning it to "Cool" for a wakener.

The first time it had happened the Centaurian had all but killed Sibyl. It was in Old Town and Sibyl had been watching a group of teen-agers at the Knockout Dropout, keeping an eye on which Centaurians came and went and which teen-agers looked as though they might be on benzale.

And she saw the Centaurian staring at her strangely and decided he was the first vicious-looking Centaurian she'd ever seen. What was there about him? When he got up for another drink, in the light by the bar she saw there was a greenish tinge to his scales.

Sibyl put on chartreuse underwear because green was on her mind, pulled filmy green stockings up below her knees and rouged both knees rather vulgarly.

The Centaurian had followed her out of the bar, and then half a block down from the Knockout he'd suddenly got one hand over her mouth and the other around her neck and pulled her into the overgrown yard of a deserted house. Sibyl put her fingers to her neck, remembering the ropy tentacles of the greenish Centaurian's hand.

She'd bit through the hand over her mouth. Bit to the hard cartilage and when the Centaurian let go she smashed his stomach with her fist and then, when he went down, pounded his head against the gatepost and left him.

Sibyl slipped into her green wool dress – it was low-cut and the diagonal weave of the skirt did things for her hips. She meshed it up the front, pressed on the vacuum cups of her green glass earrings, pressed a fake emerald bug onto the bare part of her right breast.

Scaley Moe would like that. She combed her fantastic hair quickly, so that the stripes fell into place, painted her slighty-too-ample mouth with a flat green that made her eyes shine like a cat's and wished there were time to do her fingernails green.

Well, there wasn't. She wanted to see Llanr and get to the C meeting and sometime in between she'd have to eat and work on that passage in Thucydides. Someday, Sibyl thought, someday I'll write that book on Plataea. And meanwhile the reading for it made the busy, complex world she operated in disappear.

Oh, the perfume. She sprayed on a fruity Type Three behind her ears and behind her knees.

Time, six o'clock. Sibyl clicked out a couple of pieces of bread, reached down the salami and thought about how some year she'd go back to Plataea, pace off the conjectural temple of Hera, and see where the heroon of Leitus probably was. She opened Book II of Thucydides to the account of the Theban attack on Plataea.

And remembered her honeymoon in Greece, standing on the stubbly rocky field where the town of Plataea once stood. And Kenneth's arm around her waist, and looking northward through the luminous Greek sunshine toward the battleground before Plataea, and then turning, trying to hold on her absurd straw hat in the billowy wind, and looking up at the looming might of Mt. Cithaeron.

Had she ever been so young? Thinking that she'd probably have four children, and teach, and do a new translation of certain passages in Thucydides.

And remembered trying to explain to Kenneth what was so wonderful about the scrubby couple of acres they were standing on, while he kept saying, "But the battle was over *there*."

And since then there had been so little time for Greek. She'd started out with a fill-in job while Kenneth finished up his Ph.D., and then it was something to do while she was carrying Missy, and then she kept on because she got interested; and then when Kenneth's expedition was lost on Radix, she had to work for a living. And work hard and well.

Sibyl sighed, propped her Thucydides on the bookrack, took a bite of her salami sandwich and began reading about how a Plataean named Naucleides and those with him opened up the gates to the Thebans.

When she got to the part where the soldiers grounded arms, she got up and checked the lining of her purse for her needle-thin knife, and made sure the silver rouge case really was her gun. The gold one was knee rouge.

Then back to Thucydides, and just as the Thebans were getting lost in the streets of Plataea in the dark and rain, the telephoned buzzed.

"Yes?"

"Patrolman Stanley Rauch. Lieutenant Brandt wants you at Public School Number Thirty-one. Tenth and Box Avenue. Female, age about seventeen. Looks like another benzale murder."

The police call switched off.

Missy's school!

Sibyl felt a cold pressure in her stomach. It spread up to her lungs and made it almost impossible for her to breathe. It couldn't be Missy. Missy had left only an hour ago. Less than an hour ago. And for the gym at Beman High.

Those greenish Centaurians. Would they be striking at her through Missy? Dear Missy who'd managed to almost rear herself, and who was all that Sibyl had of Kenneth. Ridiculously, Sibyl thought of a drawing Missy had made at the age of three, of a kitten with legs all around it, like a centipede, and big, gentle eyes.

Oh, Missy.

The bodies in these murders...

But surely if it were Missy they'd have said so. Or prepared her in some way. Unless they didn't know...

Sibyl found a taxi and got out into a cold wind with night brewing in it. There was a cop at the door; and one room, on the second floor, was lit up.

Sibyl didn't need to flash her card at Stanley Rauch, who was minding the door, and she went on up. Heavy police feet were walking around. As the stairs eased her to the top, her eye caught the extra light of a photographic bulb. A door closed and the doctor came out.

"Don't go in there," he said to Sibyl.

But Sibyl went in, stiff-legged. Choked with relief that the corpse was not Missy, then with nausea at what had been done.

"I expected more blood," she said, looking away from it "But there isn't, is there?"

"Yeah. No," said Lieutenant Brandt. "Here, hold the end of the tape measure over by the window. Yeah. That's what it's been with all these. Very little blood."

"Perhaps the heart had stopped beating before any wound was made."

"No. The veins were gorged with blood. They sealed themselves off. Like the others."

The body had been slashed amateurishly through the clothes, and a wound gaped just under the ribs on the right- hand side. Rusty blood ringed it, and there was blood on the hands of the girl.

Sibyl knelt beside the girl, trying to think it wasn't real.

That calm young face and that horrible wound. "What did Doc say?" she asked.

"The usual thing. The slash is the work of an amateur but the liver is neatly gone. And she didn't bleed to death. She died from not having a liver."

The photographers were finished and Sibyl pulled the sheet up over the girl. She glanced about the room. Locked from the inside. No weapon.

"There's blood on both sides of the door handles. The air cleaners have taken most of it off."

Sibyl pulled out a cigar. "Whose blood?"

"Hers. Her fingerprints. And yet there's no weapon and her liver is gone."

"Could she have come here alone after the wound was made? Did Doc say?"

"Ordinarily, no," Lieutenant Brandt answered. "But there's nothing ordinary about these benzale murders. And we never have any witnesses. Only victims."

Sibyl started to light her cigar, and then stopped and sniffed.

"I've been aware of an odor since I came in." It was very faint, but she'd smelled it before. She'd smelled it at deaths like this. The odor

8

of death? "What is it?"

Lieutenant Brandt shrugged, tested the window. "There was a faint odor of benzale when I came in, but I don't smell it any more. Stand over by the door and hold the tape measure." He walked to the other side of the room, scribbled in his notebook.

"Any idea who she was?" Sibyl asked, walking over to him with the end of the tape measure as it wound back into the spool.

"Not yet. There was no purse or—" He stopped, because Stanley Rauch came into the room and said, "This gentleman came over from across the street. He thinks he might have seen the victim before her death."

A tall, oldish Black man came in behind Stanley.

"I'm Professor Dietrich," he said. "Mather Dietrich and I live across the street and—good Lord!" he cried as Lieutenant Brandt pulled the sheet off the body. "I know that girl!"

"You're her teacher?" Brandt asked. He sat down at one of the desks and flipped over a page in his notebook.

"No. I teach at the University. English. My son used to take her out. Her name is Bella Kale. Not a pretty name." "When did you see her last?"

"Last night I happened to notice someone going into the school. I thought it might be a teacher—they occasionally come in at night to put papers through the grader and what not."

Lieutenant Brandt shifted uncomfortably. He was fat and the desk was too small for him. "What time?"

"Probably about ten o'clock."

"Think back now. Did you notice anything about the girl? Anything at all?"

Dr. Dietrich thought a moment, looking painfully down at the girl and slowly shaking his head. "I thought she was a teacher. She didn't have the springy step of a high-school girl. Yes, I believe she was walking slowly."

"Which direction was she coming from?"

Again Professor Dietrich shook his head. "She was going up the sidewalk that leads to the steps. That's all I saw. All I noticed."

Brandt nodded. "Thank you, sir. We'll have to go over all this again tomorrow. You're not under suspicion. I have to ask questions."

9

The professor walked slowly out.

"Then," Sibyl said, "she was killed after she got in. But where?"

"Nothing in the building," Brandt said.

"That smell in the air," Sibyl went on. "It wasn't benzale. It was something else."

Brandt shook his head. "Benzale angle again. The professor said he thought the girl used it. Does the name mean anything to you? Bella Kale."

"No. Aren't the Feds getting anywhere in Centaurus? Llonan City? I mean on the benzale trade?"

"Nowhere at all, last I heard. The Centaurians won't cooperate. They can't understand what's wrong with benzale. They don't think benzale smugglers are criminals."

Sibyl sat down at one of the desks, rubbing her thumb across the glassy plastic. "Then what about Stuart Grant? The man that owns the ships. After all, they're his ships now that old Page Grant is dead, and I gather he takes a lot of detailed interest in his work and goes back and forth to Centaurus."

"Stuart Grant," said Lieutenant Brandt, "we don't touch with a ten-foot pole. Besides, he's cooperating with the Feds a hundred per cent and he's already so rich the two-bit benzale trade would hardly be worth it to him."

"I read somewhere that he's planning another expedition to Radix."

Lieutenant Brandt looked around for somewhere to put out his cigar, gave up and ground it out on the floor. "Look, we know from Stuart Grant's expedition last year that Radix is nothing but a mass of vegetation. Mr. Grant looked for survivors of the first expedition, and I understood it was proved there were no survivors."

"I know," Sibyl said. "I just mentioned it. It's been ten years since Kenneth's expedition was lost there. Just about the time Centaurus was opened up. They hoped the one around Alpha Centauri would prove as fruitful. Well, Kenneth's gone. I'm used to it now." The air cleaner was slowly taking the grease of her thumbprint from the desk.

"Are you? Most women would have remarried."

Sibyl stood up. "I don't want to be tied down," she said. "This Stuart Grant? What's he like?" Somehow, there seemed to Sibyl a sort of magic and mystery about the name. Probably, though, he was just a dry, unpleasant little businessman.

Lieutenant Brandt shrugged. "I don't know anything about him but what I read in the papers. He's young — fortyish — rich, apparently a financial genius. I think he's still got the same wife he started with but there's something wrong with the marriage. He's got yachts and jets and mansions, but he's no playboy. Takes an interest in Centaurian culture and speaks Centaurian like a native."

Sibyl watched the ashes and cigar bits floating off into the draft of the air cleaner. "I always thought," she said slowly, "that there was something wrong with his report. About Radix. He brought back pictures of vegetation and soil samples and air and water samples. But... there was no explanation of what killed my husband and the rest of the expedition. And why they disappeared, ship and all."

Lieutenant Brandt frowned uncomfortably. "I thought he said they surmised the ship crashed and burned up. Or maybe never got there."

"Steel doesn't burn up."

"It could melt down and get overgrown. Mr. Grant couldn't go over the whole planet inch by inch."

Sibyl sighed. "I know." She glanced at her watch. "My God! It's past seven and the C meeting is at eight. I'll see if I can get anything about Bella Kale. There was a ship in from Centaurus yesterday and I want to meet the new Centaurians. Yesterday... has anybody checked the arrival of Centaurians with the occurrence of these murders?"

Brandt shook his head. "I'll do it. Dirty Centaurians!"

Sibyl worried at the emerald bug on her breast and then pulled it off. Somehow it seemed malevolently inappropriate. "Lieutenant Brandt," she said, "you are prejudiced and I hope you know it. It's ridiculous the way everybody treats Centaurians like nineteenth-century immigrants. Thirty years ago, when Page Grant made it to Centaurus and brought the first Centaurian back to Earth, everybody knocked each other out to proclaim the glories of Centaurian culture and to wonder at the discovery of another humanoid civilization. Now these glorious Centaurians live in a ghetto in the only merchant spaceport in the world. Think about it a little."

Lieutenant Brandt frowned, bit at the cuticle on his thumb. "After

I finish thinking about these benzale murders."

"No. It isn't fair to call these benzale murders. I can't prove anything yet, but I'm positive the benzale rings themselves have nothing to do with the murders. It's sort of... tangential to the benzale trade."

"What do you have to go on?"

"Hunches."

Brandt grimaced. "Women," he said with some disgust.

On the way home in the taxi Sibyl thought with regret that now there wouldn't be time to talk with Llanr before the meeting. Scaley Moe. Sibyl smiled at the thought of him. And besides Scaley Moe, there was someone else she wanted to talk to. Stuart Grant. Did somebody like Stuart Grant go about surrounded by an armed guard? Or could you just pick him up like any ordinary man? One thing she could be sure of. He *wasn't* any ordinary man.

Sibyl glanced at her watch as she got out of the taxi. Seven twenty. Not much time. She'd have to change and take the sidewalks to Old Town. This time on a Saturday night they'd be crowded and she might have to wait for a space. And she didn't want to keep Jimmy lurking around outside of the dilapidated old C house.

Poor Jimmy. He really thought this was the way to fight anti-Centaurian feeling. He didn't know the Centaurians came to the meetings mostly to meet girls. And to encourage interest in benzale smoking.

But some new element was creeping into the Centaurus- benzale rings. Something no one recognized as yet. Unless Scaley Moe — well, she'd see.

Sibyl let herself in the door and thought immediately about Missy. She washed off her make-up, undressed and let some youth creme set on her face while she punched the number of the Teen Center where Missy would be working out before the game. Apparently nobody there had heard about the murder. Not yet. Sibyl didn't mention it. Mostly she'd wanted to hear Missy's young, clear, live voice.

She changed clothes and put on her blue contact lenses and her light brown wig. Fortunately it would be dark and smoky at the Centaurian meeting. The youth creme worked pretty well, but it didn't last long and Sibyl felt worn and tired and the wrinkles would come through anyhow.

She worked a pair of dirty low dogs on her feet, wrapped herself into a sack shirt, wiped the excess cream off her face, put in the cheek-pieces, and looked in the mirror, trying to make her eyes look like someone who hadn't just seen a corpse. Someone who hadn't been a widow and who hadn't a sixteen-year-old daughter to worry about for whom the depths of death, desire and fear were years away.

Then she shrugged, laughed the vacant laugh of youth and took off.

One-way windows and silencers left the place looking like the other unreclaimed houses in Old Town, but the door had a "C" scrawled on it in red chalk.

Jimmy stepped out of the shrubbery and said, "Hi!"

Sibyl hooked her hand through his arm and watched as he importantly opened the door with his C key and said, "She's O.K.," to a scrubby little man inside smoking a benzale cigarette.

"No, thanks," she said to his proffered tin, "I smoke cigars."

Jimmy giggled. "But that's right," he said. "Don't ever try a benzale. They're all right for Centaurians, but I don't do it and I don't want you to, either."

They went up the stairs into a blast of Centaurian music and into a smoky, overheated room.

Somebody sloshed a drink on Sibyl, apologized, and introduced her and Jimmy to a new Centaurian who spoke with such a ferocious accent that Sibyl decided to try her Centaurian on him while Jimmy went off to find them a fizz.

"Ah, but you learn Centaurian in school, indeed?" the Centaurian asked.

"No," Sibyl answered. "I've been doing it as a special project. I think Centaurians are just fascinating."

"I think Earth ladies are indeed sweet-smelling," the Centaurian said. "So far I am here one day and I see none of the prejudice I was led to expect."

"That's because you've only been here one day."

Jimmy came back with the fizzes and put one arm around her and extended the other to shake hands with the Centaurian. They started a long, dull conversation about anti-Centaurian prejudice and what to do about it.

Standing there, watching Jimmy and the Centaurian with the ferocious accent, Sibyl suddenly began to feel the small hairs on the back of her neck rise.

Someone behind her was staring at her.

Moreover, the smell of death was in her nostrils; the faint, almost familiar odor that had been in the classroom with the dead, mangled girl...

She swallowed a rising hysteria, opened her purse, palmed the silver rouge stick that was such an efficient little gun, and turned.

CHAPTER II

Looking at her with an expression of greed, repulsion and lust was the greenest-looking Centaurian Sibyl had ever seen. He was smoking a benzale, and as she returned his look he opened his mouth and the heavy, blackish smoke curled out through his long, pointed teeth and up around his narrowed, reptilian eyes.

Sibyl smiled gaily, switched her rouge stick to the other hand and extended her right hand to him as she made her way across the room.

"Hands across space," she said girlishly, and flapped her eyes at him.

"Hands, indeed," he replied.

"You are a recent arrival?" she asked.

"Yes. Only yesterday."

"Business?"

"Of a sort. Mostly I'm on vacation. My wives are getting old and my nerves need a rest."

"You speak excellent English," Sibyl said.

"Also French, Russian and Italian. To a Centaurian these languages seem much alike, though I know it does not seem so to you. Our fresh approach makes many things possible."

"They're interrelated languages," Sibyl pointed out.

"So wise for your age," the Centaurian said with a touch of irony. He knew who she was and he knew she knew.

Sibyl reached over, on an instinctive impulse, and took the cigarette from his snaky fingers.

She took a puff, to keep it alive, but didn't inhale.

"Let's you and me get out of here," she suggested.

The Centaurian looked surprised. "Sure," he said. "O.K."

As soon as they were in the dark, the Centaurian's rubbery fingers were on her mouth, and he had her neck crooked in his elbow. She back-slashed him with her heel, stooped down and brought her shoulder up into his ample stomach, so that he went over face first and his teeth cracked on the sidewalk.

The cigarette still burned in her hand. She walked on two blocks to the outskirts of the new city, hopped into a taxi, and took her first inhalation of a benzale cigarette. Only this wasn't quite a benzale cigarette, she was sure. It was where the faint, odd smell had come from. The smell in the room of the crime. The smell of the greenish Centaurian.

The effect was fast. Faster than she'd expected. Already she felt a slight dizziness.

"Hurry, driver," she said. "I'll pay the fines."

She was home in two minutes, tipped the driver a dollar, ran up the moving steps to her apartment in case the elevator was occupied, and threw herself down on the bed inside. She could hear herself breathing and an ache crept up from her right shoulder, probably from the weight of the Centaurian she'd thrown. She began to be a little scared. Would it do any good not to smoke any more of the cigarette?

But she'd gone this far. The cigarette was only half an inch long now, and Sibyl poked it into a bobby pin and smoked it quickly down until it fell apart and the bobby pin scorched her fingers.

I'm a fool, Sibyl thought. This is no way to find out what the effect of an off-brand benzale cigarette is.

But how else was she going to find out?

Will I turn faintly greenish? She wondered. She'd never seen a greenish human — only greenish Centaurians. The blood chemistry was somewhat different, of course. That was what made it safe for adventurous girls to sport around with Centaurians.

Green girls. Would she be a green girl? At forty?

Green. "A green thought in a green shade."

"Sibyl!" called Kenneth, and Sibyl sat up and looked wildly about.

"Sibyl!" Kenneth ten years dead, somewhere lost on Radix.

"Yes, Kenneth, where are you?"

But Sibyl's body was too heavy for her. She couldn't get up. Couldn't even get herself off the bed. Her eyes felt sewn together.

"Sibyl!"

And, furious with her creeping physical helplessness, Sibyl lay there and her mind opened to the drug with a soft rustle, as a moon-flower opens to the moon.

Green. There was a taste of grass in her mouth, a smell of green and her back ate and drank at broad sunlight hungrily.

"I'm Kenneth Blue," the green said, as a man might say to himself when he feels he might be going mad. "Not green. Blue.

"At night you get hungry for the day. Hungry for the sunlight. Cold sunlight. Hot sunlight. Any flavor sunlight."

Then, abruptly, another dream came to Sibyl. This time there were no words. Only impressions that seemed to come through blurred. A sense of sudden slowing of all her processes. A change and growth. A growing into a slow movement of swaying... What? Part of an infinite growth, change...

Then that dream went and another came. This one was a seed dreaming a flower, and it was so lovely that Sibyl would have wanted to keep it forever. It blew about in her mind and then wafted off, and Sibyl dreamed herself running after it, calling, "Come back! Come back!"

...wanting to be no longer a person but an endless green dream building endless forms of itself and there being no Sibyl Sue Blue, but only...

Sibyl screamed and waked with a sense of utter desolation, utter horror. As though she were going mad alone in the dark. She ran her hands over her head. Her body. Something alive was inside of her, going through her veins, *eating* at her. She could feel them. Streams of parasites.

She turned on the light, went over to the mirror and was amazed to see she didn't look any different. Except for her own expression of horror. She was so conscious of something within her! It was so real and so conscious that she was actually able to push the thing from her mind — her brain. To expel it, bit by bit, and feel it go into her blood stream and feel where it was, going through the valves of her heart, through the large arteries.

The benzale effect, she thought. The feeling of power and self-confidence. The release of full mental and physical potentiality.

Yes, but the other, the parasites... they streamed through her, and now they all were piling up at one point in the right side of her body, just under her lungs... the parasites. There had never been any description of this as part of the benzale effect.

If they all collect in one place, Sibyl thought, then they can be got rid of. She stood up, closed her eyes, feeling a knot they made in her right side. And pain. It began to be very painful.

There was a sudden ringing of the doorbell. No! Sibyl checked the door to be sure it was locked. She must be alone.

She went into the kitchen, found a carving knife. The parasites must be got rid of and she must be alone. There was no room for thought of anything else. The pain got worse. A knotted fist of pain, so that she couldn't stand up.

Someone was knocking at the door now, insistently.

Sibyl put the knife to her side. Then, "Sibyl!" It was Kenneth's voice in her ears. "Sibyl, beware!" And then a consciousness of Kenneth, as though he grew along her veins, within her mind. And the knot in her side began to loosen and Sibyl felt a blackness come over her mind.

The last thing she heard was the insistent knocking, and someone shaking the door, trying to get in.

Sibyl waked up in bed. She opened her eyes and then closed them quickly. The light was on and it hurt her eyes.

Her lids felt dry and sore and the bed was like a furnace. She pushed the sheets off painfully, turned away from the light and sat up.

She put her hand to her arm. "Something stung me," she said. She felt drunk. The room kept changing size. It looked enormous. And then when she blinked and looked again it looked tiny, like a doll house.

She felt the bed sink on one side. "Mother," Missy said, touching her with a cool hand. "You're sick. Lie back down."

"The light hurts my eyes."

Missy switched off the bedside light and switched on the one by the dresser.

"I gave you something to bring the fever down," Dr. Mason said from nowhere.

"Fever?" Of course. She was sick. When had she gotten sick? The last thing she remembered was...

"I want to examine you," Dr. Mason went on, "before I shoot you full of antivirus and antibiotic."

She had been trying to save herself. Radix was engulfing her, and then it was all streaming into her liver. Radix? How had she known all that? Or thought that? And thought that it was necessary to excise it, to operate on herself... but then there had been Kenneth's voice to stop her. She hadn't known what to believe, what to do. But the knife... and Radix?

"Missy," she said, "where did you find me? What was I doing?"

"Take a deep breath," Dr. Mason said. The stethoscope was icy cold.

"You were on the kitchen floor," Missy said, "with a knife in your hand. Your clothes were cut. Like you see. You were muttering, but you were asleep. I called Dr. Mason right away."

Missy sat on the vanity bench, her dark hair bunched on top of her head as she did it for basketball, her foolish-looking gym suit dirty and rumpled. She looked a little scared.

"Did anything else happen? Did I *do* anything?"

"No. Except call Daddy's name. But there was a man who was trying to get into the apartment when I came home. He tried to insist on coming in but someone came walking down the hall and I started to call out and the man went away. He said he had to see you. Then after I got in, and I guess when the hall was empty, he came back, rattling the door and asking for you through the door hole when I went to see who it was. It wasn't until Dr. Mason buzzed from downstairs that he went away. I had called Dr. Mason as soon as I found you on the kitchen floor."

"Did you see anyone, Dr. Mason?"

"No. Open your mouth. Wider. He probably went down the back escalator. Try not to gag."

"Sorry," Sibyl said. She felt cooler already. She liked the expert touch of Dr. Mason's hands on her neck, knowing that if there were anything wrong he'd be able to find it "What did the man look like,

Missy?"

"Swallow," commanded the doctor.

"He was a sort of smallish, thin, dressed in something dark and dignified; all I remember well is that he had very thin eyebrows and looked as though he ought to be bald — like a baby — only he wasn't."

"Then he wasn't a Centaurian."

"Oh, no. And he had an educated voice. I guess that's all I can describe about him."

Dr. Mason clicked his instruments away into his black bag and smiled his nice smile. Never professional. "I can't find anything at all wrong with you, except a typical benzale aftereffect. I'll take a blood sample and call you in the morning. Take aspirin if the fever comes back. Why did you smoke a benzale cigarette?"

"Because... well, it's part of a... hunch... I'm following up. More than just a hunch now. The cigarette I smoked had something added to it. I wanted to see the effect. That blood sample — would it show if I were infected with a parasite of some kind?"

"It might. Depends on the parasite. More likely you mean a virus. There are certain tests for certain viruses. Why?"

"I was wondering if it were possible to detect a parasite or virus from another planet."

"Centaurian X-I has been isolated and studied. So far that's the only one."

"But suppose it were an entirely new virus from an entirely new planet?"

"Centaurus is the only new planet we know about. The other planets of the Centaurus system are not habitable and have not been explored."

"I'm talking about Radix."

"Radix! You mean the one Kenneth was lost on? *Very* unlikely you'd have any such virus. Though there was an expedition last year, wasn't there?"

Sibyl nodded. "Stuart Grant — *the* Stuart Grant — made it."

"Well, you don't exactly sort viruses out like peas," Dr. Mason said. "But I'll see what the virologist says."

"Hand me a cigar, Missy, will you, and mix me a gin and 'gin." Sibyl sat up in bed, hugging her knees and feeling unaccountably good. A thrill at being alive. "Dr. Mason, would the fever be part of the benzale aftereffect?"

"Definitely not. And Missy, get me a gin and 'gin, too. Do you know it's pouring down rain outside? I'm chilled clear through."

Sibyl smiled. "You *could* get a younger doctor to make your house calls for you."

"Younger!" Dr. Mason indignantly blew out the match he was holding for Sibyl's cigar. "I'm only ninety-two."

"You're wonderful," Sibyl said. "That's why I instruct my congressman not to vote for socialized medicine. I believe you know everything there is to know about medicine and a lot besides."

Dr. Mason took his drink from Missy and looked mollified.

Sibyl sipped her gin and 'gin and enjoyed watching Dr. Mason and wishing he were forty years younger. "Tell me," she said, "about viruses. Could a virus carry a... message?"

Dr. Mason laughed at something in his own knowledge. "In a way," he said, "that's all a virus is. A message. Or rather a set of instructions."

"But I mean *literally*," Sibyl said.

"I mean literally, too. Picture a virus as a... oh, perhaps a round, hard, lifeless bead, infinitely small, smaller than a bacterium. Say it's floating around in the air and somebody breathes it in. Then the little bead lands on a nice, damp, suitable cell and suddenly something starts to happen. It pokes a little needle into the cell, the contents of the bead goes into the cell and the dry husk falls off. Now this is where it gets interesting. It doesn't start reproducing inside the cell, devouring the cell like a bacterium. Oh, no. It simply acts as a gene in the cell. It orders the matter of the cell to turn *itself* into a bunch of viruses. It actually changes the genetic behavior of the cell."

Sibyl set her glass down, breathing deeply. "This is *fantastic!*" she said.

"All of science is fantastic. But this is nothing new. Viruses have been studied for over fifty years."

"I mean the implications for me are fantastic. Now look. Could a virus — theoretically — instruct a cell to make not more viruses, but a different kind of cell?"

"Oh, yes." Dr. Mason stood up and walked over to the window.

"The rain is beautiful," he said. "The light catches it and it unrolls like so much tinsel. And people ask me if I still find things to enjoy at ninety-two... Yes, it is certainly possible for a certain type of virus to go into a cell and another type come out. In some cancers a virus has caused genetic damage. In others the very process you're talking about may have occurred. A virus turning a normal cell into something else."

Sibyl got out of bed, unconsciously holding closed the knife rip in her blouse. She pursued Dr. Mason as though she were pursuing knowledge. "But do you think it would be possible—theoretically—for a virus to go into the brain and carry a *thought*?"

Dr. Mason raised his eyebrows. "A nerve virus? I don't know. That's a harder question to answer. So little is known about the chemistry and physics of the thought process. But I wouldn't put it down as impossible."

Sibyl let out a breath. "Fantastic!" she said.

"No more fantastic than the rain," said Dr. Mason. "Thanks for the drink. I've got to get back home to watch 'Brave Dr. Andrews' make all the nurses in the tridi hospital. Marvelous program."

Sibyl walked to the door with him. "I'll bet you used to make all the nurses at the hospital."

"*Used* to!" snorted Dr. Mason. "Ha!"

Sibyl went back to the bedroom and admired Missy brushing her hair. "I'm glad you came home after all," she told her daughter. "But I thought you were going to spend the night out."

I was. With Margaret Schliemann. But I found out there'd been a benzale murder at my school and I wanted to know if you knew and maybe help you. The girl was in my class. Bella Kale. She was... oh, sort of shy and retiring and I didn't know her well. But still... who would do a thing like that? To a girl like that? And *why*?"

I don't know yet," Sibyl said. "But suddenly the benzale aftereffect is gone and the gin and 'gin has me feeling all golden and slumbery inside and I think I'll just go to sleep. Don't let *anybody* in that door, honey."

Sibyl awoke in the depths of night to a telephone that had been ringing a long time. It had left lightning forks through the darkness of her mind.

She got up groggily and switched it on, tucking the button in her ear so the conversation wouldn't wake up Missy. It was Lieutenant Brandt. "Oh boy," he said. "Oh boy, did *you* manage to stir things up. What's the matter? Were you drunk?"

Sibyl was still trying to swim out of the oceans of her sleep. "What did I do? Tell the truth, I'm still half asleep and I don't remember—"

"Come immediately to headquarters and be prepared to answer questions. I'm at a C meeting at the moment. You are reported as having disappeared in company with a vicious Centaurian. Helpless little you. A youth named Jimmy Stour is having histrionics about it and members of the League for Centaurian Equality are out for his blood for calling the police during a C meeting where benzale is being traded about. Then the Centaurian—a big beast of a Centaurian named Rrinn—accused you of man-handling him and he's got broken teeth to prove it. We've got to arrest him for carrying benzale cigarettes and I've got a million teen-agers to question and even so, some got out—probably carrying benzale."

"I'll be right there." That idiot Jimmy!

"You go to headquarters."

"No. If Rrinn's given any teen-agers those benzale cigarettes of his I think we'll have another murder."

Sibyl thumbed off the telephone and got herself a cup of coffee and took out a fresh blouse. Maybe Jimmy would know who Rrinn had given cigarettes to and where they might have gone, in case they got out before Brandt got there to confiscate the cigarettes.

Sibyl smeared on her youth creme quickly and straightened her wig. Something in those special cigarettes brought suicide and... murder? Sibyl should have gone straight back to the C meeting. Why hadn't she thought of that right away? After the dream?

She went out into puffs of light rain and taxied to Old Town. The C house sounded noisy now, with the front door open and a knot of curious people watching the police car and Stanley Rauch at the door and people milling about on the inside stairs.

"It's me," she told Stanley, flashing her card and lifting her wig briefly.

"This time I know," Stanley said admiringly.

Sibyl went on up and Jimmy was so glad to see her he almost

cried.

"I'm sorry if you were worried," Sibyl said, feeling like a real fink. "I went outside with that Centaurian for some fresh air and somebody hit him so I ran, I should have run back into the C house but it was easier to run the other way so I did and I took the sidewalks home. Then I thought I ought to come back so I hired a taxi and the door was open so it looked safe and I came on up."

"If you'd only give me your phone number," Jimmy groaned. "Or tell me where you live. When you disappeared I didn't know what to do. Where to start calling or anything. So I called the police and now it's a real mess, with the benzale and all. And everybody thinks I'm anti-Centaurian because I called the police. Oh, Sibyl!"

Sibyl hated herself. Jimmy would get over this, and her, but it would take a long time and it was a dirty trick to use him like this. How can you walk through another person's life and not break things?

"I told you about my family," she said darkly. "Jimmy, did that Centaurian give anybody cigarettes? Or sell anybody cigarettes?"

"I guess," Jimmy said. "They're arresting him. He's got this wild story about *you* beating him up. He's crazy, I think. He tried to resist arrest. Look at the brute!"

Two hefty cops flanked Rrinn but he wasn't trying any rough stuff now. He was talking earnestly to Lieutenant Brandt.

"Jimmy, I've got to talk to the police. If he was saying things about me, I've got to defend myself. No, I'll go by myself."

Lieutenant Brandt was bringing Rrinn into the hall, where the telephone was. Sibyl followed them, closing the door of the hot, bright room and enjoying the cool dimness of the hall.

"I didn't *say* you had to answer questions before you call your lawyer," Brandt was saying in an irritable voice.

Rrinn was glaring at Sibyl, his hand on the telephone. "The Centaurian League is going to bring charges against *her*," he said. "And I refuse to make my telephone call in her presence. She is both brutal and incompetent. Her disguise is laughable."

"You knew about it," Sibyl said. "You recognized me somehow. I'd like to know how." She turned to Brandt. "By the way, where are the cigarettes you confiscated from this delicate little flower?"

Brandt frowned slightly, pulled a tin out of his pocket. It was a typical benzale tin—a Centaurian ointment box with a garishly carved lid and a false bottom for the cigarettes. Sibyl sniffed each cigarette separately and carefully, then replaced them all.

"Benzale," she said, with some relief. Then Rrinn had not been distributing the off-brand wholesale. But had he distributed *any*? "By the way," Sibyl asked, "where were you last night, little lotus?"

Rrinn looked around, as though surrounded by witnesses. "Here," he said. "Here we were welcomed by the Terran Committee for Centaurian Equality."

"Whatever you're getting at we can go into later, Sergeant Blue," Brandt said. "You might as well leave the hall so Rrinn can make his telephone call. I want to get this over so I can go home and get some sleep."

When Rrinn came out, two cops carted him off, but Sibyl stopped Brandt before he went out into the hall again. "Who did he call?"

"Somebody named Beadle. Never heard of him before."

"Beadle? I've heard that name somewhere before—I associate it vaguely with Centaurians, though it certainly isn't a Centaurian name. Where?"

"I don't know. I haven't. It was supposed to be Rrinn's lawyer and he's supposed to meet us at headquarters. But it sounded to me like there was something fishy about it. Maybe not. Some of these Centaurians just sound like that. Odd thing was, the Centaurian mentioned the name of someone he'd given a benzale cigarette to."

"One name?"

"Yes. But I've got three others he also gave cigarettes to."

"But the important one is the one he called Beadle about. Don't you see? That's going to be the next benzale murder!"

"No. I don't see. But we'll have Rrinn locked up and he can't commit any murders."

"Who is she?"

"The girl? Her name's Gracia Joad. And she's disappeared."

"You mean you don't know where she is?"

Brandt made a face. "I didn't mean she went up in smoke. Several got out before we got someone around to watch the rear fire escape and the side French windows. These old houses have a thousand exits."

"Beadle," Sibyl said ruminatively. "You know, if he isn't a key person in this whole thing, I'll eat my cigar." And lighted one. "Look, I'll take it upon myself to see to Gracia Joad."

"O.K.," Brandt said unwillingly. "But don't do anything except locate her and then call me. I don't want you doing anything else active on this case until we have a chance to clear things up. Maybe you need a rest. And if the C League brings formal charges against a member of the force it's going to make a stink from here to Llonan City."

"Check," Sibyl said, leaving that worry for later. "You take the rest of my cigar. Sweet little things like me don't smoke cigars."

She pushed through the door into the remains of the C meeting, where indignation was rising as the police were leaving.

"Did they search you like that?" someone was saying, and Jimmy, looking pale, was standing alone in a comer.

Sibyl took his arm and led him out. "No use standing here to get crucified," she said. "It was all my fault but they'll blame you. Look, do you know a girl named Gracia Joad?"

"Who doesn't?" Jimmy said. "I mean if you're a boy. She's not the kind of girl you want to know."

"That isn't important. We've got to find her. I think she's in danger."

"She's the kind can take care of herself. She usually goes by the Knockout Dropout on a Saturday night. You know."

The Knockout had Centaurian music that swirled down the block at them, and lattices of light that changed color dizzily. A Centaurian at the door welcomed them in and offered a tray of fuzzy pink Centaurian wine. Jimmy dropped two quarters on the tray and he and Sibyl pushed through a shrieking crowd that was watching a Centaurian do his clumsy dance in the middle of the floor.

"I don't see her," Jimmy said. "But in this crowd—"

"Isn't that Kally Bond?" Sibyl asked. "The one you said she left with?" He was an auburn-haired, thickset boy with the slightly desperate look of those who know they're going to spend most of their lives getting into trouble.

They pushed their way through the crowd to Kally, who sat on the floor sunk in his black corduroy overalls as though they were a house in which he lived alone.

Sibyl scrunched down next to him. "What happened to Gracia Joad?"

He looked her over carefully and flung an arm around her. "Went to the Ladies'. Didn't come back. You'll do."

"Did she smoke a benzale cigarette?"

"Yeah. Think so. I didn't. I don't like to feel energetic. Look at that fool on the dance floor."

"Yeah," Sibyl said. "Did... do you know a girl named Bella Kale?"

Kally looked around at her. "No. How come you're so interested in me?"

"Just a passing fancy," Sibyl said. She got up and made for the Ladies'. There was a man in it. A thin, oldish- looking young man in an impeccable business suit.

A girl was there, crushing out a cigarette on the floor. She had on yellow lipstick and yellow eye shadow and her frizzy auburn hair was tied up in yellow ribbon.

Sibyl bent over and picked up the cigarette butt and sniffed it. That was it, all right.

"Are you Mr. Beadle?" Sibyl asked the man.

The man eyed her coolly and didn't answer. He had baby-thin eyebrows and looked as though he ought to be bald, but he wasn't. That was Missy's description of the man who had tried to see her when she was having the benzale dream. Radix dream. He flicked a glance at Gracia Joad.

"Then of course you're the plumber," Sibyl said. "Come on, Gracia. I got some news for you. Important news."

"What kind of nut are you, Tootsie?" Gracia asked. "I don't know you from nowhere."

"That cigarette you just smoked is poisoned. You'd better get right to a hospital." It wasn't going to do. What could she tell the girl? What would she believe?

Gracia went out of the door with the man following her. "Now finish telling me why you were looking for me, Rollo," she said to him.

"My name isn't Rollo. And I wanted to talk to you alone. I'm connect with... a theatrical agency."

As they went by, Sibyl grabbed Jimmy's arm and whispered,

"Keep them here. Do anything. I've got to make a phone call."

At headquarters Brandt didn't like it at all. "Suppose this is all your imagination," he said. "We'll look like a bunch of fools."

"And just suppose it isn't? Then what'll you look like? I tell you, the man here is Rrinn's Beadle. Has his lawyer showed yet?"

"No. There hasn't been time. I'll send a patrol car over. There's one at Tenth and Oak. We'll pick her up on a benzale charge. But if she doesn't have any on her, we can't hold her."

Sibyl buzzed off and looked around for Jimmy. He was standing alone at the door, looking unhappy.

"I tried to tell her she was in danger," he said miserably. "But she only looked at me. To tell you the truth, she suddenly looked drunk. Her eyes got glazed while she was standing here and he took her down the street. Look!"

The man was helping Gracia into a car and she did, indeed, look drunk. He looked up to see Sibyl and Jimmy in the lighted doorway of the Knockout, shoved Gracia unceremoniously into the Tireless Triumph, and hurried around to the driver's side.

"Come on," Sibyl said, running. They hopped onto the rear bumper and climbed to the top of the car and clung to the luggage racks.

CHAPTER III

"Rollo" started off with a lurch, then slowed to turn a corner. He went on cautiously, a careful, fussy driver. Then a police siren sounded and he lurched forward and began to drive crazily around a jumble of streets, as though to throw off anyone who might be following him.

Sibyl cursed herself silently for not having asked Brandt to leave off the siren. Rollo headed for open country, down the main highway. Occasional headlights beamed at them through the light drizzle of rain and they passed the last of the neon-lighted roadside stands and the rain got darker and wetter as they sped along. Sibyl couldn't tell how far they'd gone.

Beadle turned down a side road, to the left.

"I don't like this," Jimmy said, for the fiftieth time. "Maybe he'll slow up and we can jump off and go back and call the police. This is something for the police. Maybe she's not drunk. Maybe you were right about the poison and she's dying. Then what will we do?"

Sibyl shivered, hung on tighter. The road looked like old asphalt in the headlights. With the Tireless Triumph it wasn't possible to tell whether it was a bumpy road or not. She couldn't find any way to identify it, remember it.

As the car turned right, Sibyl thought she saw a saggy barbed-wire fence and wooden posts. There was a brief crack of lightning, showing a desolation of earth and sky, and the rain swept down harder. Sibyl could feel Jimmy shivering.

"I told you to get off," Sibyl said. "When he stopped for lights in town. Now I don't know how you'd get back. And if Gracia is dying, I'll need your help." Dying. She might be. Every minute counted. Sibyl tried to remember her dreams. How long had they taken? How long before the unbearable pain in her side and the urge to excise it. She didn't know how long. It had seemed hours but it hadn't been, because she hadn't been gone from the C meeting that long and she'd had the doctor in and slept besides. Maybe it was half an hour, forty-five minutes.

Time! She could feel it going by with the beating of her pulse, with the tempo of her breathing.

The road seemed to be ending. No. It branched. The driver took the left-hand fork, then turned right a little further on. Sibyl was utterly lost. The road grew so narrow she could almost reach out and touch the trees on both sides of the road. If those dark things clashing in the flapping rain were trees.

Finally the Triumph slowed. There was a dim light ahead, shining sadly through the rain. Up close, it lighted the doorway of what appeared to be an enormous old barn, with an even larger structure of some kind looming behind it. The bare, old wood was soaking up the rain, and the door — a plank of old, age-grooved wood — opened.

"Help me get her out quickly, Hatty," the driver of the car said. "The Centaurian was arrested and he called me, the idiot. I don't like it. Tell Stuart—"

The hulking man in the door said suddenly, "What's that on top of your car?"

With the engine off and the rain temporarily stilled, Sibyl had been hearing Gracia moaning. Hatty came over to look and Beadle walked around to the light.

"A knife!" Gracia screamed, "I need a knife." She was rattling her door, but apparently it was locked on her side.

Sibyl slid down the dark side of the car, pulling Jimmy with her, and shoved him into the back seat while she got into the front.

"There's somebody there!" the man named Hatty said.

"There was that woman," Rollo said. "She—"

But Sibyl had the ignition on and spurted off in a circle. It was a single-lane road they had come through and she wanted to come out frontways.

"Stop!" the hulking man shouted. "I'll shoot!"

A bullet sped by the window. The rain splattered sharply again. Were they shooting to kill, or only to stop Sibyl and Jimmy? Gracia

30

was beginning to writhe slowly. Fortunately there were no tires to shoot holes in.

"Down!" Sibyl cried to Jimmy, pushed Gracia down with her right hand. The gun barked again, again, and bullet struck metal. She almost missed the path into the road, wasn't sure it might not be a cowpath, the narrow parting between the trees. But she plunged down it anyway and kept going, feeling her heart pumping wildly up under her Adam's apple.

"Jimmy, do you have any idea where we are?"

"No," he answered. "What's the matter with Gracia? Is she dying?"

"I don't know. There's just a chance... we've got to get her to a doctor as soon as possible. There's a bare chance that a general antivirus might do the trick. Which way do I turn if this road ever ends?"

"I don't know. I'm really lost. Maybe we better just get as far away from that barn as fast as we can. Do you think it would do any good if I gave Gracia artificial respiration? I think I could do that."

"No. It wouldn't do any good. I believe I should turn left. We mustn't end up just going around in circles. I'll have to go it by ear."

"I didn't know you knew how to drive, Sibyl," Jimmy said in a funny voice.

"I know," Sibyl said. "Please... we'll go into all that later. Keep an eye on Gracia."

Gracia was doubled up, not screaming now but moaning. "Please let me out," she said over and over. "I'm going to be sick. I must be alone. I need a knife. I'm in pain. Oh, please!"

The dark drive through the rain went on endlessly and now Sibyl saw lights through the rearview mirror. Someone was behind them, catching up quickly, someone in a car with tires, that bumped up and down in ruts, the headlights approaching unsteadily. Someone that knew the road and didn't have to hesitate. Sibyl speeded up, tangled in a thick crop of bushes on the side of the road, tore out dragging a big bush by the roots, had to slow for the third turn. The headlights behind her got brighter. But she thought she could hear distant truck tires on a highway.

"I think we're getting there," she said. She could hear in her mind the sound of Gracia's life going away. If there were only some way to *hurry*. But even with the rain letting up it was so dark!

Then she could see highway traffic to her right. She speeded up just a little, took the road to the right. A bullet, shot from too far off, hit the back of the car and slid off. The gun fired again, missed.

A sudden rush of relief washed over Sibyl when she reached the highway. Here, at least, was the outskirts of civilization, of reality. It was like coming out of a nightmare. She glanced briefly at Gracia, who had now started ripping at her clothes with something she'd found in her purse. Either a pencil or a nail file.

"*Watch* her, Jimmy!" Sibyl shouted.

Jimmy reached over to the front seat and grabbed Gracia's hands. "She's strong," Jimmy said. "You better hurry."

The car behind was almost upon them now, and shooting again, but the highway was busy with returning weekend traffic and once she was on it... Sibyl had to wait but she was afraid to wait. So she leaned on her horn, darted across the highway, turned in a lay-by, pulled off a large hunk of red highway mud and took the fender off a large, old Buick that was trying to get out of her way.

Then her motor stalled and the Buick's driver, a squat, ugly-looking man boiling with rage, started toward her using language that must have made Jimmy's ears turn cerise. The car ahead stopped and two adults and five very sleepy-looking children got out to watch the fun.

Jimmy cried, "Watch her!" and lunged for Gracia a little too late. She had taken her knee rouge case and calmly shattered the shatterproof windshield. Blood ran down her arm.

"What the *hell* is going on here?" the squat man asked.

"Need help?" the couple from the family car yelled cheerily.

Sibyl reached furtively for the ignition. It worked and she took off. She hoped they'd call the police, but she couldn't wait.

Jimmy was hanging on to Gracia and she was struggling hard now.

"You're all funny, Sibyl," Jimmy said, his voice breaking a little. "Here you are driving and all and your voice—"

"I'm afraid there's a lot you don't know," Sibyl cut in. She realized that she'd forgotten for some time to disguise her voice. "We're taking Gracia to headquarters and I'm going to make a report. This case is about to blow sky-high. Gracia is the proof I need to start with."

"And you," Jimmy said, "you're not Sibyl?"

"Oh yes, I'm Sibyl. But I... you can come on into the bright lights of the police station with me. I'm sorry. And some time when this is over I'll explain it all in detail to you. Keep a tight hold on Gracia."

The car was following them now. A sleek, black Dalmation. But nobody was taking a chance of doing any shooting in the city. When Sibyl stopped in front of the police station the Dalmation went smoothly on. Sibyl memorized the license number and let it go.

"Get a doctor!" Sibyl shouted to the cop standing under the misty light in the entrance. "Quickly. Anybody. No. Doctor Mason. He'll understand better. Tell him we need an antivirus."

She handed Gracia to the second cop. "Keep hold of her until the doctor gets here. Her name is Gracia Joad. Have somebody be trying to get hold of her family. Look in the City Directory. Her mother may have remarried." Somehow Sibyl pictured Gracia as having a succession of weak-willed fathers.

She looked down at the perspiring, pain-twisted face of the girl. All tinseled with her ribbons and make-up and so young now.

Sibyl started past the desk and remembered Jimmy. He stood awkwardly by the door, looking at her in the dull, fly-specked illumination of the police station.

"Come on in, Jimmy," she said.

In Lieutenant Brandt's office Sibyl pulled off her wig, popped out her contact lenses and lit a cigar. "You were wonderful, Jimmy," she said. "You were brave and helpful all the way and I'm sorry I had to get you into all this."

Jimmy looked at her in the merciless light of Brandt's office and turned pale. He ran his fingers through his hair and bit at his lip. "I was wonderful," he echoed. "You... and you were... Yes, ma'am," he finished.

"Never mind," Sibyl said. "I'm going to introduce you to my daughter. She's better at explaining things. If you'll wait out there someone will get your report on tape and then you can go home and get some sleep."

Jimmy went out, silent.

"Now, what *is* all this?" Brandt asked from around a dead cigar. "You've already kept me up most of the night."

Sibyl gave him the high spots. "And when we were at this barn of a hide-out, Rollo — Beadle — started to say, 'Tell Stuart...' So you see we've got to get onto Stuart Grant. Remember he just made the second expedition to Radix last year."

"I don't see what that has to do with it. And there are plenty of people named Stuart."

"But you can't rule it out."

Brandt measured a pencil carefully in front of his eyes and then balanced it in the middle. "You can't rule out the president of the UN, either. I tell you the Feds have investigated this man. He had nothing to do with benzale."

"This isn't benzale," Sibyl said insistently. "All right, I'll — "

"Doctor's here," Bill Cluny said, opening the door.

Sibyl rushed out grasped Dr. Mason's hand. "Listen. Whatever I had and recovered from somebody else has and isn't recovering. My virus came with something to fight it. Something only I could trigger off. It's the virus from Radix. Can you do anything for her?"

Sibyl led Dr. Mason into the cell where Gracia lay doubled up on the cot, her eyes closed, no longer struggling. "Feel her liver," Sibyl said. "It shrivels the liver. It's a 'benzale murder.' Only not completed."

"Get her clothes undone."

Sibyl got her knife out of her purse and slit Gracia's clothes open while Dr. Mason opened his black bag and put his stethoscope around his neck. His hands flew rapidly over the girl and he shook his head. "Lump like a stone," he said. "I think it's too late for anything but we'll give it a try. I hope you've got the same type of blood. If not, it'll take hours to get a serum from yours." He drew the needle out of Gracia's arm, pulled something out of his black bag and took it all over to the light. "Be getting blankets on her immediately," he said. "She's in shock."

"Blankets," Sibyl called to Bill, and pushed up her right sleeve.

"It's O.K.," Dr. Mason said. "You're a B but she's an O. But let me do a quick agglutination."

"Sounds like a lot of bad language to me," Sibyl said, hardly feeling the needle as he slid it in. She pressed the cotton pad as he slid it out.

"It might be just as efficacious to do a rain dance," he said, shoving the slide he'd prepared under his microscope, "but I'm going to try your blood for a vaccine. I'll also give her a general antivirus. I'm too old not to be willing to try anything."

Bill had brought the blankets and Sibyl tucked them carefully around Gracia. And kissed her lightly on the forehead and patted her hair into place. Gracia's skin was ice cold.

"I'll be in the next room taping up my report," Sibyl said. "Call me if she becomes conscious. Or if there is anything I can do."

Sibyl walked over to the desk. "Anything on the parents yet?"

"Yep. Mother and stepfather. The stepfather's drunk but the mother's on the way."

Jimmy was sitting on the bench against the wall, looking lost and glum. "I'll get Bill to take you home in a patrol car," Sibyl said. "And stay home. I don't think you're in any danger but don't take chances. And don't go to any more C meetings for a while. And... thank you."

Jimmy just looked at the floor.

Sibyl got her report on tape, stretched, lit a cigar and decided that if her eyes closed she'd never get them open again. She looked up at the window and saw a pallid dawn oozing into the sky.

Brandt looked in. "I'm leaving," he said. "I'm falling asleep at my desk. The Joad girl is coming around. Rrinn is still under lock and key."

"Did you find any more benzale on him?"

"No. I'll read your report tomorrow. Or rather this afternoon. You go home and get some rest and I'll call you when I need you."

Gracia was surrounded by her mother, two police matrons, the police surgeon and Dr. Mason when Sibyl came out. The mother was sobbing loudly.

Dr. Mason moved nimbly over to Sibyl. "I don't believe it after having felt that lump," he said, "but I think she might come out of it and her liver feels normal already. Her temperature shot up but it's not dangerous."

"Thank God!" Sibyl sighed. "Now look, I want you to take some more of my blood and keep it in case something like this occurs again."

"Come by the office —"

"No. Now," Sibyl said. "Something could happen to me on the way home even."

Dr. Mason got his bag and took the blood, poured a colorless chemical into it. "This isn't the way to do it," he said, "but in a pinch I might be glad I did."

Sibyl got Bill to take her home, just in case that black Dalmation was lurking around the comer waiting for her to come out. She looked in on Missy, who was sleeping soundly, and went soundly to sleep herself, too tired to even wash her face.

Fourteen hours later Sibyl was in the bar of the Stilton, trying to pick up a young millionaire named Stuart Grant.

It was easy to see which one was Stuart Grant. Nobody else was that tall and broad and wore diamond cuff links unless they posed for after-shave ads, and he didn't have that kind of expression on his face.

He looked bored.

Three overdecorated blondes were trying to cheer him up. One of them was his wife.

"With apologies," Sibyl muttered, "to God, Home and Mother," and waded in.

She kicked the two blondes who were not the wife in the shins and shouldered the wife politely aside.

She straightened her black chiffon cocktail dress so that most of her left breast showed. "I'm Sergeant Blue from homicide," she said to Stuart Grant.

"And I," he said appreciatively, "am the teen-age werewolf. Well, where are the cuffs?"

Sibyl smiled calmly, reached into her smart but capacious handbag and brought out a pair of handcuffs.

She snapped one onto Stuart Grant and one onto her own wrist. Hers was especially made to fit her fragile-looking wrist.

The millionaire grinned. Sibyl tugged and he followed.

"For God's sake!" the wife said, and downed another straight bourbon.

"She always says that," Stuart Grant said, and followed Sibyl into the bar next door. It wasn't as plush as the Stilton, but it had sound absorbers hanging from the ceiling and soft pink lighting that brought out the best in Sibyl's complexion. And it was plush enough so that it had personal service and No Centaurians Allowed — without a sign being necessary.

"Quite a gimmick," Grant said. "Bourbon and water with a lemon jack."

Sibyl undid the handcuffs because in a minute he'd be annoyed with them and then it wouldn't be cute any more. "Gin and 'gin,'" she said. "It wasn't really a gimmick. If I'd had to use force I would have."

"I'm not sure I want to find out what all this is about. But I'd sort of like to see you using force. I've never been raped."

Sibyl absorbed his six foot two of bone and muscle, the strong, watch-strapped wrist and the curl of black hair on his forehead. "Don't tempt me," she said, and handed the bartender her credit card.

"Oh, come on," Stuart Grant said, flabbergasted. "I'm a millionaire."

"Yeah, but I'm on an expense account. Anyway, I like to start out with my criminal at a disadvantage, Mr. Grant."

"Stuart." He incontinently licked all the lemon off the top and then swallowed a bit of the bourbon and water disinterestedly. "You?"

"Sergeant Sibyl Sue Blue. Sibyl to you."

He frowned. "Sergeant! You don't really mean that, do you?"

Sibyl pulled her card out of her purse.

Stuart read it incredulously. "I haven't committed any murders lately. But if the police want to question me, why don't they call me in?"

"This is more fun, don't you think? Anyway, I find out more like this than with the bright lights and bamboo splinters."

"Shoot then." He was looking at her closely with those brilliant hazel eyes, and Sibyl found herself almost uncomfortably aware of his maleness. When she looked briefly away and then back he was grinning at her just a little. He reached over and pushed a lock of hair back over her right ear. The little gesture evoked a startling emotion in her, and she reined herself in quickly.

"Well, there is a curious, coincidental relationship between Centaurians, benzale rings and... you."

"Me!" Stuart curled one side of his mouth disgustedly. "See here. If it's a matter of the benzale being smuggled in on my ships, we've been cooperating with the police about that for years."

"I know. It has to be your ships because there aren't any other ships. That isn't it."

"And if it's the antitrust suit, that's in the hands of good lawyers on both sides. I don't want a monopoly. But I'm also not going to give away any of my hard-earned ships and nobody can afford to compete with me."

"I know that, too. But didn't you see my card? It says 'homicide.' I got transferred after the first benzale murder."

"Then why are the police after me?"

"Not the police. Me. Nobody suspects you of anything. It's just that I've been thinking... no doubt there's no connection... but the first of these peculiarly horrible deaths occurred a year ago. And a year ago was when you came back from Radix."

Stuart raised an eyebrow and looked... disgusted? Bored? A little frightened? Sibyl couldn't read it. "A year ago," Stuart said, "there was also a lot of sunspot activity, there was a heat wave in Tibet and an outbreak of smallpox in Rhodesia. Have you investigated all that yet?"

"I know." Sibyl finished her drink and signaled for another. She wished she could be enjoying the dim, liquor scented bar and the faint background throb of music with this very appealing man, instead of... "I know how you feel. But look at it this way. All the juveniles that were murdered — and in that peculiarly horrible fashion — had some tie-up with the sale of benzale. Now, benzale itself certainly doesn't incite anyone to murder. It never has, and it has been widely used and experimented with for years before there were any murders. And the kids that were killed — it wasn't for money or even benzale, because none of them had any, not when they were killed, anyway. And believe me, despite the wave of anti-Centaurian feeling that all this triggered, Centaurians don't have a brutal, murderous streak. We've never found a Centaurian murderer."

"So you conclude what?"

"I don't know. Hunches. Mostly I concluded I wanted to meet you. Who wouldn't want to meet a big, handsome man like you?"

Stuart lit a cigarette, frowning handsomely in the little flare of the electric heat. "Well, now, if you put it like that, let's discuss something more wholesome than benzale murders. Sex, for instance."

"Ah. You have a hobby. Yes, but first—I can't help wondering, in a vague sort of way, if you might have picked up some sort of... oh, germs or viruses or sublife on Radix. Without knowing it, of course. And I remember you landed on Centaurus before you came to Earth. Which would make the germ or virus or whatever a secondhand import from Centaurus."

Stuart softly whistled out a stream of smoke. "Any sublife I have," he said, "is my own. If you read up on my expedition in the papers and in the scientific journals, you'll find out all about it. You picture a monstrous, amoeboid germ going around with a knife and slashing teen-agers?"

Sibyl thought of telling Stuart what she knew about the Radix virus, and then decided it might be too soon and too dangerous. She smiled instead. "Well, then, I'd love to hear, from your own lips, what Radix was like. Very green?"

"A whole planet just green. Overgrown with jungles—not trees, really. Big, odd plants."

"For instance," Sibyl said, "even perhaps plants that possess some sort of intelligence? And plants that can change their own genetic make-up if they feel like being a different shape—or even a different substance?"

Stuart laughed. Was it a sincere laugh? "You certainly have hunches when you have them," he said. "Have you ever wondered whether they were just dreams?"

"Suppose," Sibyl said slowly and seriously, "I said they *were* dreams."

Stuart peered into his glass. "It's a funny thing," he said, "but the women who look like they're going to be the most interesting always turn out to be neurotic. And if there's anything duller than a sober woman, it's a neurotic woman."

"Suppose I brought you a certificate from my doctor to prove I'm not neurotic. And then suppose—I have a vacation coming up—suppose I volunteered to go with you Friday on your second expedition to Radix."

"*You!*"

"Me."

"Look," said Stuart, shifting his weight around on the back of the padded bar seat. "This has gone far enough. You're kind of cute, for your age. But you presume a little too much. If the police should want me for anything, they can get me." He turned the seat and shoved himself off. "Better luck next time, baby."

"O.K.," said Sibyl. "But I've got two things to say to you. The first is that if I get bumped off by any green Centaurians, the cops will be more suspicious than I've been able to get them so far. And the second is, that if you see my husband on Radix, give him my regards."

Sibyl handed him her social card with *Mrs. Kenneth Blue* on it. Stuart gave her a hard stare, took the card, stiffened at the name, bit his lip and left.

Sibyl finished off her gin and 'gin pensively, retrieved her credit card and waved off an uninteresting-looking man with a convention button on.

This wasn't going on her police account. It was her own private account. The down payment on a cruise to Radix.

Sibyl let herself in her apartment. "Missy?"

"Studying," Missy called from her room.

"Any calls?"

Missy came in, holding a finger in a book. "There's one on the answer box. Your boss. You look beautiful."

"Thank you. I didn't do too well on my last interview. I keep having the feeling I was saying either too much or too little."

"Oh, and Dr. Mason called. He said to tell you Gracia Joad is going to live. I think that was the name."

Sibyl nodded.

"Then a man named Beadle was here. He said he'd be back but I wasn't to tell *anyone* but you. He also said it was very important. And mother, he was the same one who wanted to see you last night. When you were sick."

"Whew!" Sibyl said. "This case is dropping open like helicopter blades. But I've got to talk to Scaley Moe before I see Beadle."

Missy worriedly lost her place in her book and ran a hand through her hair. "Mother, I really don't think you ought to see that Beadle fellow alone. I don't like him."

"I know I oughtn't to see him alone. But I can find out things that way that he'd never tell me if I had a big cop here and hauled him down to the station. Brandt's got his boys out looking for Beadle now. And I only hope they don't find him yet. Who won the game last night?"

Missy relaxed a little, smiled. "We did. And I had a good time at the low dog afterwards."

Sibyl began unmeshing her tight black dress. It was a gorgeous dress, reserved for special dates only, but it wasn't near tacky enough for Llanr. "Missy, I hate to ask you this because I know it's a lot of trouble, but I want you to go live with Auntie for a while. You can help her with the children and she'll be only too happy to have you. She says you mix the best gin and 'gins in town."

Missy frowned. "I don't mind getting out of the way when you need me out. But if it's a matter of danger, I'd rather be here." Missy followed her mother into the bedroom.

"It's a matter of a lot of things, This 'benzale murder' is coming to a head now. And... I may go away Friday. For a long time. There's another expedition to Radix." Sibyl paused for a moment and looked at Missy. "I'm going to go if I have to hide in the explosion chamber."

"Radix!" Missy looked incredulous. Then she said, "Father didn't come back."

"I know." Sibyl straightened her black dress against its friction hanger and got out the green one. "I got all this on last night for Scaley Moe and then I never did get there. I'll call and see if he can come here before I go getting all dressed. I know Kenneth didn't come back. But the next expedition did. And... two things. Have you eaten?"

"Eaten?" echoed Missy, as though it were a foreign word. "No. I had a big malt about three o'clock."

"Well, would you heat the oven and stick in a couple of those chicken and burgundies I made last week? They're in the freezer. Marked 'C and B.' And I'll be calling Scaley Moe and then I'll tell you why I want to go to Radix."

Sibyl slipped into a robe and punched Llanr's number on the telephone.

Scaley Moe's clipped, nasal voice answered before the first ring had stopped. "Discount Centaurian Imports," he said. "Scaley Moe at your service."

"Sibyl Sue Blue at your service on this end, Llanr. It just occurred to me that I haven't seen you for a long time and here it is Sunday night and nothing to do."

"Ah, Sibyl," he said. "My pretty little friend. So roundly made. I was going to call you; I have something to warn you about. But not on the telephone. Perhaps you could meet me at Joe's Bar, or some other sweet-smelling rendezvous."

"I think you'd better come to my apartment."

"With great pleasure," said Llanr with a pleased snap of the teeth. "But you've never told me where it is."

Sibyl gave him the address, hung up and went into the kitchen to put a quick salad through the chopper.

"Mother," Missy said worriedly, watching the dinners bubble softly in the little electronic oven, "are you all right? I mean—you haven't been through the Schenthal medical computer in a long time."

"Honey, if there were anything wrong with me, Dr. Mason could tell by looking at me. No, I haven't suddenly gone off my nut. Curious how everyone thinks so, though." Missy raised the glass lid of the oven, waited for the heat to go out, removed the dinners and set out knives and forks.

"I've got good and sufficient reason to think it's a bug from Radix, passed on by certain benzale cigarettes, that causes the suicides that look like murders. The virus affects the brain, runs through the body and then settles in the liver, where it encapsulates the liver cells entirely and neatly seals it off from the surrounding tissues and blood supply and what not. Then somehow—and I think it has to do with this Mr. Beadle—this encapsulated tissue is taken away. But the really important question is *why* is this happening and how long will it go on."

Missy handed Sibyl the blue cheese and the salad tongs. "Then it isn't because of my father that you want to go to Radix?"

Sibyl mixed the dressing, crumbled the cheese over the salad and tossed it gently. "The chicken smells wonderful, doesn't it? Just that pinch of rosemary does it."

"That and the wine."

Sibyl suddenly found out she was starving and ate voraciously while she talked. "It's on account of your father, too. This virus: you remember how I smoked that benzale cigarette—one of the funny kinds—and I had the fever and everything? Well, the virus, or rather the extra virus that was activated by being in my system—the virus contained a sort of... message... from Kenneth."

Missy drew a sudden breath. "Mother, you can't really believe that. Oh, *Mother!*"

"Ordinarily, no. But if the virus can carry a dream of Radix, which it does—then why not also something from Kenneth, who was lost there? I mean, it's only slightly less believable. And Missy, it's enough for me."

Missy ate, more slowly now. "All right," she said. "Is Scaley Moe coming here or are you meeting him somewhere?"

"Here. I've finished eating and I'll go start your packing for you. The checking account is in both our names. Use what you need. And of course Auntie and Jack will see to your inheritance if... if it should become necessary. Don't cry, Missy. I intend to come back."

"So did Father."

"Yes, but this is the third expedition and the second one *did* come back. I think I could get back for you if I had to fly across space in my nylon slip. And speaking of slips, I'd better start your packing and my dressing."

Sibyl packed underwear, socks and stockings and bedroom slippers, which Missy would forget, and left the rest for Missy to pick out. Then she got into her green wool dress, the little fake emerald bug, green earrings and a lot of make-up. Then she called Kenneth's sister and helped Missy find enough clean blouses and her one hat.

"You have your key, Missy. Come back next week and get anything you need. The rent is paid for the next quarter. And Missy?"

"Yes?"

"I know how hard it is right now to be you. I... I'll tell you the secret of life right now. Quick. The secret of life is for you to enjoy being you. If you can do that, everything else happens by itself."

Missy laughed. "Mother, you *do* manage to find the right things to say and I love you. Have a good trip."

Sibyl emptied ash trays, cleaned the table quickly, switched on the electronic air cleaner briefly, sprayed herself with a deluge of smelly perfume.

The doorbell rang and Sibyl opened the door to Scaley Moe's broad, ugly, friendly visage.

CHAPTER IV

"Hello," said Sibyl.

"Hello and hello, indeed," Llanr returned, and stepped into the vile cloud of perfume around Sibyl. His face lit up into an appreciative leer. "Ah, what a sweet-smelling apartment you have. Everything so feminine."

"Have a cigar," Sibyl said, "and come sit down."

"I have my benzale cigarettes. Since you haven't put me in one of your delightful jails yet, I assume I can go on smoking them when I am with you. Tell me," he went on, poking Sibyl's emerald bug with an interested tentacle, "is that pinned through your well-rounded member?"

"Later," Sibyl said. "I'll show you how it works. Right now I want to have a little chat with you."

She led Scaley Moe over to the sofa and sat down next to him. Odd how Centaurians smelled like stale cigar butts, when what they smoked was benzale. Still, Sibyl liked the smell of old cigar butts.

"Ah, a chat," said Llanr, edging closer to her. "Then you have heard rumors? Such an unpleasant subject."

"Rumors? No. I mean, what kind of rumors? Wait. I'll get you a drink and I want to hear the news, pleasant or unpleasant."

She brought whiskey and water and lit a cigar. Llanr took a long, rather noisy pull at his drink.

"Well," he said. "Well. You mustn't hold it against me if I am a bringer of bad news. There is a delegation of Centaurians going to your superiors to complain that you show unreasonable prejudice against Centaurians and that you use brutal police methods."

Sibyl smiled at Scaley Moe and leaned back against his shoulder.

"Do you think I'm brutal?" she asked. She liked Llanr. Maybe he wasn't the prettiest, freshest thing the Lord ever made, but he was nice and Sibyl liked to be appreciated the way Llanr liked to appreciate.

"No. But I think you're in danger of being brutalized, you delightful-smelling creature." He kissed her lushly. "They say you beat up three Centaurians."

"I did," Sibyl admitted, straightening her hair a little. "But they hit me first. Look, Llanr... No, we've got all evening and you *wait...* I want to know if you've noticed any difference in Centaurians within the last year."

Llanr released one arm, picked up his drink and finished it. A vein pulsed darkly along one temple of his delicately scaled forehead. "Only what I told you. This recent anti-Earth, or rather anti-Sibyl talk."

Sibyl got up and mixed more drinks. She didn't want to say too much to Scaley Moe, because he wouldn't keep it to himself. On the other hand, she needed to question him, and you can't ask a question without showing something you know or suspect.

She set down the tray with the two drinks and eased herself down close to Llanr, thinking what strength she drew from being close to a man. Any man, since it couldn't be Kenneth. But she blocked Kenneth out of her mind.

"Haven't you noticed," she asked, "that some Centaurians now have a... greenish tinge?"

"Of course. Chlorosis. There has been a high incidence of chlorosis in Llonan, our spaceport city. But it is not a serious disease and it goes away by itself. It has no connection with Earth, except that it was first noticed by an Earth doctor on Centaurus."

"You mean all those Centaurians hadn't noticed they were turning green?"

Llanr shrugged. "You didn't know? We are almost color-blind, by Earth standards. That's why we wear color combinations that you people sometimes find so shocking."

Sibyl mashed out her cigar thoughtfully. "What else do you know about chlorosis?" she asked.

"Nothing. As far as I know no one goes to a doctor with the disease. It goes away and does no harm. Like a sunburn, maybe."

"But what causes it?"

"Who knows? Who cares?"

"Then do you know who the Terran doctor was?"

Scaley Moe put his arm around her and kissed her on the forehead as lightly as Centaurians can kiss. "All this idle conversation," he said. "But all right. I happen to know about him—and thus hear about the chlorosis—because he sold through me a lotion he invented which shrinks the scales of Centaurians until they look almost like human skin. A specialty product of little consequence. Most Centaurians are very vain and we think ourselves handsome the way we are."

Sibyl smiled and leaned on his shoulder. "I think so too. Sometimes I think you're the nicest man I know. What was the doctor's name?"

"Beadle," Scaley Moe said. "Dr. Wilfred T. Beadle."

"Beadle!" Sibyl sprang to her feet, spilled her drink down the side of her leg. "Sorry. It's just that—What else do you know about him?"

"All that lovely bourbon! Here, let's get that stocking off before you become chilled, you lovely, delicate creature. I don't know anything else about him. He came back to Earth from Llonan City, dropped in to ask me how the lotion was selling, and then disappeared. I've sold fifty dollars' worth of the lotion but I can't find him to give it to him. Why does his name excite you so?"

Sibyl stripped off her stocking and squeezed it out into the ash tray. "It's because I've heard his name recently. A Centurian named Rrinn mentioned it."

Llanr frowned. "Rrinn. He's the latest one you are supposed to have brutalized. But Beadle—I've heard nothing of him. Tell me, little rose petal, how do you go about brutalizing these big, fat Centaurians?"

"Oh, I manage. Llanr, are there two kinds of benzale cigarettes?"

Llanr reached over and stubbed out his cigarette with the hand that wasn't around Sibyl's shoulder. "It's funny you ask. There've been rumors about a cigarette that produces odd dreams."

"Nothing else? Just dreams?"

"In Centaurians, yes. In humans, I don't know. The reaction is different with so many things. Benzale, for instance, which produces a much milder effect in us. But these rumors—I haven't tracked them down, not being much interested. I make most of my money in Centaurian wines and crafts."

"But who," Sibyl asked, "who in particular has inquired about these new cigarettes?"

Llanr shrugged. "I don't know a name. A new immigrant or two here and there. I attached no importance to it. Next time, if you like, I'll find out the name."

"Oh, yes," Sibyl said. "That would be such a help. Scaley Moe, you are a jewel beyond price and I love you."

"I love you, too," Llanr returned in a comfortable tone of voice that meant nothing complicated. "And now show me about that emerald bug?"

"It was the Roman poet Ovid who said it," Sibyl answered, "but I don't agree. I just feel—oh, heavens, the doorbell! I'd almost forgotten. See how you distract me, Scaley Moe?"

"Would you like me to hide under the bed?"

"No. Get out the back way. It would make my visitor nervous if anyone saw him. Just scoot out the door behind the kitchen. Then you walk down the stairs at the end or the passage and there's a service elevator. This is a business call," she added.

Llanr got himself organized quickly. "Ah, all business, you delightful policewoman. Good-bye, little gleerl blossom!"

Sibyl threw on a paper house dress and ran a brush through her hair. The doorbell from downstairs stopped ringing and a few moments later there was a knock at her door. Sibyl glanced in the mirror, saw her make-up had rubbed off and decided Beadle wasn't a person to bother doing make-up for.

She slipped the knee rouge gun into her pocket and opened the front door.

"I," said the man who came into the room, "am Wilfred T. Beadle."

"Ah, so you *weren't* the plumber," Sibyl said. "Come in. I'll get you a drink if you promise not to shoot me when my back is turned, Dr. Beadle."

"I did *not* shoot at you," he said testily. "And I don't drink."

"Well, perhaps you at least sit. Do sit down."

"How did you know I was a doctor?"

"I have my sources. Why did you take a chance like this, coming to see a policewoman, when you must know the police are after you for questioning?"

"Because I know you want to go to Radix and I can help you, but not if you throw me in jail. And because I must find out why you are alive." He sat in Sibyl's rose tapestry armchair, knitting his tiny eyebrows and looking vaguely petulant.

Sibyl folded her arms across her chest and put her feet on the coffee table. "That's too broad a question. I'm alive for the sheer joy of living. Or perhaps to fulfill some divine design. Or then—"

Dr. Beadle made a motion of irritation with his mouth. A thin mouth topped with a thin mustache. "You know what I mean, Sergeant Blue. You smoked one of those cigarettes."

"And what should have happened?"

"What *did* happen?"

Sibyl uncrossed her arms, padded barefoot over to the mantelpiece to get a cigar. "Oh, come now, doctor. I'll tell you, but you've got to tell me a few things, too. Give and take. Do unto—"

"What do you want to know?" He eyed Sibyl's cigar disapprovingly.

"Let's see," Sibyl mused, unwrapping the cigar as she padded back to the sofa. "What *do* I want to know? First, is the virus originally from Radix?"

Dr. Beadle nodded. "I suppose you know that already from your dreams? Or is it true about the dreams?"

"Was it purposely brought to Centaurus from Radix?"

Dr. Beadle's mouth tightened into a white line. "That is not for me to know. Not my business."

"You seem to have your morals well compartmented." Sibyl thumbed her lighter and lit her cigar. "All right. Does the virus do what it was originally intended to do?"

Dr. Beadle sat up even straighter. "No. You've got the crux of the matter there, though I don't know how. You don't look like an intelligent woman, Sergeant Blue."

"Thank you," said Sibyl. "I've had a lot of practice. What was the virus originally intended to do?"

Dr. Beadle's mouth tensed again. Sibyl decided he was the most irritating-looking man she'd ever seen and it brought out in her a strong maternal urge to get him drunk and shake him up a little. But this wasn't the time.

"You must have had very poor toilet training," she said.

"I beg your pardon, madam."

"Oh, nothing. So you won't tell me what the virus was meant to do. Only that it didn't do it. Was it meant for humans or Centaurians?"

Dr. Beadle hesitated a moment. "Centaurians," he said.

He sat still and erect while. Sibyl smoked her cigar for a moment, thinking.

"Boy!" she sighed. "What a whopper of a blooper somebody committed."

"Now," Dr. Beadle said, "how did you escape the unfortunate fate of the others who ingested the virus?

"In just a moment. If you knew the virus had gone wrong and what the effect was, and in at least some cases — as with Gracia Joad — that was the person that was infected, why did you let them die? Or more simply are you a murderer or do you have a rationale for this.

Dr. Beadle clasped his hands in his lap. "As these unfortunate people were doomed in any case — there is no antivirus for the Radix virus and nothing to be done — provision was made to retrieve the encapsulated organ, which is to be returned to Radix. That is not my job at all. It just happened that I had to do it the other evening."

"But someone could prevent the cigarettes from being brought in!"

"No one manages to prevent the benzale cigarettes from being brought in. I have been using the virus samples I have from the victims to try to make an antivirus specific for the Radix virus. An ordinary polyvirus doesn't do it. I have been unsuccessful."

"You sure have," Sibyl said distastefully. "But then after the victim has slashed himself and this encapsulated tissue or virus or whatever is gone, the victim then gets up and walks off?"

"The victim — unpleasant term — lives for about an hour. Apparently — I don't know for sure — part of the virus effect on the brain is that the person wants to isolate himself. A fear, perhaps, though unfounded, of contaminating others. Now, I have said all that can be said. Why did you get well?"

Sibyl stood up, walked to the window to look out at the weak sliver of moon high in the sky. "I'll tell you and see what happens. Those Radix viruses—I suppose it is a complex of viruses—included a set from my husband, Kenneth Blue, who was lost with the first expedition to Radix ten years ago. They were triggered into action when they entered my system, and it was Kenneth, in this way, who fought it out of me." Unexpected tears rose into the back of Sibyl's eyes. For so long she'd not let herself think of Kenneth. Of what might have happened to him and of the courage he must have had.

"Your *husband*!" Dr. Beadle stood up, too. "But that's impossible."

"Is it? Do you know that?" Sibyl went into the kitchen to pour herself a drink and to steady her tears back. She could cry later.

She came back calmer, carrying the gin and 'gin. "Do you know that it is impossible?" she repeated.

"No, I don't. If it is possible, then I... I need to know more than I do. But you should be immune now to the Radix virus. And perhaps an antivirus could be made from your blood. Although at this point—"

"My blood was used to cure Gracia Joad. Look, you say maybe you can help me get to Radix. Maybe if you tell me all you know about Radix we can be useful to each other. You seem to feel there's something you haven't been told. Then you weren't on Stuart Grant's previous expedition?"

"No. Nor have I talked to anyone who was. There's to be an entirely new crew this time."

"And you're going to Radix, too. Why?"

"Because I have a special talent that will assist in communicating with a life form on Radix. Look here, I'm telling you too much."

"No, you aren't. You know I want to go and you know why. I'll do anything at all to get on that ship to Radix. Including cooperating with you."

Dr. Beadle pulled a square case out of his pocket. "You had a Radix dream and recovered. You're immune to its physical effects, at least. But I think we could learn a lot if you'd try again. I mean, if you'd smoke another benzale cigarette containing the Radix messages, and then tell me what they are."

Sibyl bit her lip and eyed the cigarette. Perhaps there was more to the message from Kenneth. Perhaps more to be learned about Radix, since now she knew what to expect.

She took the cigarette, lit it, and Dr. Beadle trailed her into the bedroom. "I can stay," he said, "in case you say — " He stopped and stiffened. There was a ringing of the bell.

"Don't answer it," Sibyl said.

"Perhaps I'd better not stay," Dr. Beadle said. "I mustn't be found. Does anyone have a key?"

"My daughter. But she's gone for the night. If necessary you could get out the back way." She was breathing in the smoke deeply now. The effect wasn't so immediate as it had been with the first Radix cigarette. But she thought she was beginning to feel dizzy.

The telephone buzzed, but Sibyl shook her head. The answer box could take care of it.

Dr. Beadle was looking unhappy. "I'll get in touch with you later," he said, and went out.

And his word, "later," echoed greenly in Sibyl's mind. "Later" over and over, until the word had no meaning, and she was in a green state where there was no Time. No "sooner" or "later." No things done that could not be undone. No tomorrow that could not turn about on itself and become yesterday.

And then Kenneth again. The same calling, the same green loneliness. Eyes. No eyes... the dream went on and Sibyl waked suddenly, as she had before, with Kenneth's voice calling, as if in the next room. "Sibyl!"

And a door closed somewhere.

It was a man's tread.

Tears came into her eyes. She sat over to the side of her bed, her mind colored a little still with the fabrics of her dreams. And if it *were* Kenneth, if it could possibly or impossibly be Kenneth...

"Hello, Sergeant," said Stuart Grant, his eyes shining a little strangely. "You left me your card so I thought I'd call." He was outlined in the light from the kitchen.

"How... how did you get in?"

"Oh, I have my little ways and means. Like the back door. You didn't answer the bell or the telephone and I knew you'd want to see me."

He sat down on the chaise lounge, reached over and switched on the light. He had a gun in his hand. "Do you always sleep in paper house dresses?"

Sibyl stared at the gun. Why was he afraid of her? "Not when I'm expecting such interesting company in my boudoir. If you'll get out for a moment I'll comb my hair and rouge my knees for you."

Stuart was sniffing the air and looking at the squashed Radix cigarette in the ash tray by Sibyl's bed.

"A good-looking man like you doesn't need a gun," Sibyl said. She was wondering if she could get to her own gun without arousing his suspicions. Or get close enough to clip him off guard.

" 'Seduction is for sissies,' " he quoted. "Tell me, just why do you want to go to Radix with my expedition?"

"I already told you. Besides, I think you're cute." Sibyl was edging toward her dresser, where her purse with the gun was.

"Suppose I say I don't believe you." Stuart got up and stood between Sibyl and the dresser. "Suppose we think about what curiosity did to the cat."

Sibyl tensed herself for a spring. If he came a little closer and she were lucky...

Then a blackness closed over her mind and she felt another benzale dream coming upon her. She struggled to keep her consciousness but she felt her mind closing, as she watched Stuart standing over her, the gun in his hand, the odd look on his face.

But the Radix dream came back weakly, and then her dream was strangely of Dr. Beadle's voice and a dense confusion of thoughts. And then a dream — or was it a dream? — a languid half-consciousness of Stuart's hand on her breast. And then being gathered to his wide, strong chest, and his mouth on hers and the deep cry inside her at his plunging kiss. And then a sob because he went away and left her with the agony of her longing...

And all the time something in her mind was waiting for Stuart to shoot her. Tensed for the sharp darkness of sudden death.

When Sibyl woke up it was full morning and the sun, flashing in points on her window and blazing in her mirror, was so bright it buzzed. Sibyl sat up thinking that something illogical was happening. Surely sunshine wouldn't buzz.

No, it was the doorbell that was buzzing. Someone was leaning on it. Sibyl threw off the cover—how had it got on her?—and tried to think who it might be.

Last night had seemed longer than any night could possibly be. Stuart Grant at the Stilton, with his handsome grin, Scaley Moe's heavy hands, Dr. Beadle's clipped, precise voice, confirming incredibly what Sibyl already knew, Dr. Beadle's voice, Stuart Grant's dream kiss...

Sibyl shook herself, scratched the sand out of her eyes, hated the insistent doorbell. Who might it be? There were so many people now who were involved with the Radix cigarettes in one way or another and knew that Sibyl knew. The police, Dr. Beadle, the green Centaurians, even Scaley Moe, Jimmy, Gracia Joad, Hatty at the big, old barn, Dr. Mason, Stuart Grant... Sibyl caught her breath and looked over at the bed, as though expecting to see her own body lying there with a bullet hole in it. Why hadn't Stuart shot her?

Sibyl pulled off her crumpled paper house dress—there was a long tear in it—and threw on her aquamarine robe. She got her gun out of her dresser drawer, opened the door, stood just behind it and said, "Come in."

Stuart Grant came in, gun first. Sibyl reached out and deftly chopped his wrist with the barrel of her gun. His Colt dropped to the floor and he let out a cry.

Sibyl held her gun on him and the door slammed to behind him. "Now it's my turn with the gun."

"I didn't intend to shoot you. The gun was for self- protection. And some information I wanted."

"What information?"

Stuart grinned. "I already got it."

"Did I talk in my sleep?" There was that persistent memory of Dr. Beadle's voice in her ears. But not Stuart's.

"Maybe."

"Do you know the police may be after you?"

Stuart shrugged, still rubbing his wrist. "I hear they're getting out a warrant for Wilfred T. Beadle. I regret if my associate—employee—

has been mixed up in some nefarious business. But I'm hardly responsible."

"It'll lead to you, sooner or later. Dr. Wilfred T. Beadle didn't bring that virus back from Radix. He didn't go to Radix. I heard he discovered the disease—chlorosis in Centaurians—while he was at Llonan City. I imagine it was at this point that you whisked him off to work for you."

"He has a special talent I need on Radix, and it has nothing to do with viruses. And how, may I ask, is it possible to tell that a virus is from Radix? Do you expect them to find passport stamps on it? A virus is the size of—"

"I'm literate, too. Look, I haven't even had my coffee yet. Go away and we can chat through your bars later on."

"There aren't going to be any bars, whether your speculations are airy or not. Tell me, do you still want to take that vacation on Radix?"

"So you're planning an escape. And telling a police-woman while she's standing here with a gun pointed at you. Suppose I say no and thumb that telephone and get a couple of big cops out here? Or even shoot you myself?"

But Stuart had found out something, or decided something, that made him different from last night.

He answered her with a nonchalant lift of his eyebrows.

"And suppose I say yes?"

"Then I just might take you with me."

"That's fine. Only there are a few things I've got to know. And you either tell me or I thumb the telephone and have you brought into the station for pulling a gun on me last night."

But Stuart's look of self-confidence was unshakable. And the gun in Sibyl's hand just made him grin whenever he glanced at it.

She moved a little closer to him with it. Damn him! What *was* there about him? He was more dangerous unarmed than he was armed. She wished she knew whether that kiss last night was real. And that she could look at his mouth without remembering it.

"I haven't had my coffee yet," she repeated. "That makes me nervous and my trigger finger might develop a twitch."

"You wouldn't really shoot me, would you?" And he stood looking at her as though he were probably going to kiss her and something began to rip inside Sibyl and she thought, oh, Goddamn it, I'm going to fall in love with this man.

He knew that, and he was doing it on purpose and he was going to use her and she wasn't going to be able to stop and she cried, "Oh, I *hate* you," and tried to pull the trigger, but she couldn't. And cast about in her mind for something to hang on to. Something to save her. Kenneth. Dear Kenneth. Long, long dead. Yes, that was why she wanted to go to Radix. *Was* Kenneth dead?

She put the gun down and drew her hand across her forehead. "Yes, I want to go to Radix with you. I ought to shoot you. Or get a big cop up here while I have my gun on you. But I want to go to Radix. And I also want to know what this virus is and what your interest in Radix is and why you had those murders committed, because you did, didn't you?"

"No. It was all a product of Radix."

"Radix is a planet."

"Tell me why you want to go there." Stuart had quietly picked up his gun. Sibyl didn't care. She'd made her choice.

"Because," she said, "because I think my husband may still be alive. And also because there is some reason why this virus is being used. Perhaps even you don't know." Sibyl went into the kitchen, turned on the fire under the coffee. Stuart followed her, putting the gun away somewhere under his coat. How normal he looked. How handsome and reassuring and... nonalien, his hair still damp from the morning combing and his fine, dark hazel eyes regarding her with such interest.

Murderer?

She handed him a cup, carefully not touching him. As if he were quicksand into which she might fall. And struggle helplessly.

"You seem to be an awfully devoted wife," Stuart said with a trace of sarcasm. "Still, it's a good indication that you can be single-minded when you want to."

"I think you like to be enigmatic." Sibyl watched the strong cords of his neck, the flexure of his arms under his suit coat. There was such a feeling of controlled power about the man. "Are you going to tell me why you set those green Centaurians on me?"

Stuart looked genuinely startled. "Set... I did nothing of the kind.

What do you mean?"

"Every time a green Centaurian sees me he has an overwhelming desire to kill me. But if you really had wanted to get rid of me, that's a pretty stupid way to go about it."

"Do you really think I'm stupid?"

"No. But then why set them on me?"

Stuart worried at his coffee with his spoon. Coffee didn't interest him. "I don't know. But I'd like to. I don't like this at all."

"I don't much care for it myself."

Sibyl took a sip of her coffee, slipped the cellophane off a cigar, flapped off the end, lit it and blew a cloud of blue smoke. "Can you smoke cigars on spaceships?" she asked, thinking suddenly that she could face giving up her life with equanimity, but if she had to give up cigars, too, it might be more than she could bear.

"No. It's all very wholesome." Stuart drained the last of his coffee, lit a second cigarette. "Beadle's got something to give you so you don't twitch when you give up smoking. Let's go."

"Now? I thought you were leaving at the end of the week."

"I've pushed it up to tomorrow, and if you're coming, you've got to come now."

"Running away?" Sibyl said.

The telephone rang. It was Lieutenant Brandt. "Hi, hon," he said. He never called her "hon," and Sibyl tensed. "You're being pulled off the benzale murders."

"Tell me the rest of the good news before I start yelling with joy," Sibyl said, getting her cigar out of the ash tray.

"Well, you haven't been reassigned yet. Just have a little vacation. Only stick around in case we need you."

"Uh-huh," Sibyl said. "O.K. Couldn't I take just a *little* trip for my vacation?"

"As a matter of fact we'd rather you didn't take even a little trip."

"That's what I thought. There wouldn't be any Centaurian pressure to take me off the job, would there?"

"If you insist," Brandt said, "you can report in and I'll draw you pictures. Only like I said, don't take any trips."

"Is the Joad girl still O.K.?"

"Yes. And there's nothing to show any connection between her and Rrinn."

"You mean you *still* don't believe me?"

"I didn't say that. You're getting your vacation a little sooner. Usually that makes people happy."

Sibyl switched off and stood there a moment, looking through Stuart blankly. "I don't see how I can leave," she said. "I haven't convinced Brandt."

Stuart took her by the shoulders and used his eyes on her. Then he tilted her chin up, put his arms around her and kissed her. Softly, this time, but insistently, and held her body close to him. "Please," he said, breathing under her ear. "I want you."

Sibyl swallowed, tried to slow her breathing, tried to call her mind back, away from the stir of erupting emotion Stuart called forth. She turned away a moment, bit her lip, composed her face with an effort.

"What do I wear?"

"You can wear a G-string."

"I'll be more comfortable in a tailored suit," she said. "Get yourself some more coffee in the kitchen."

She dressed quickly, packed a small bag with extra underwear and blouses and a couple of throwaway dresses. She sat down in front of the mirror to do her hair and a quick make-up job. And looking at herself was taken aback by the intensity of her own stare. She sat still a moment, barely breathing, looking into her own eyes and realizing that there was still something unsaid in her mind. Something... Almost without realizing it Sibyl was hypnotizing herself.

"Sibyl!"

"It was Kenneth's voice.

"Sibyl! Sibyl!" The voice throbbed in her ears, and she let it fill her mind. "Danger. Alien culture. Murder. Alert Earth. Sibyl! I'm trying. I alone... It's..."

There was a pounding on the door and the thought shattered. "How long does it take to put on that G-string?" Stuart called. "I've been thinking about those attacks by green Centaurians and about that call from Brandt. I don't think we ought to hang around."

Sibyl brushed her hair quickly and painted her mouth, That would have to do.

"Besides," Stuart said when she came out of the bedroom, "I

loathe waiting around for women to dress. Remember that!"

Sibyl refrained from telling Stuart that she loathed men who treated her like a favored headwaiter. She switched on the answer box and started a note to Missy.

"Where could Missy call me?"

"At my home. All sorts of business goes on there. I have a switchboard. But tell her if my wife answers, hang up."

"Sounds real cozy." Sibyl penciled a note quickly to stick in the outgoing mail.

"She doesn't understand me," Stuart said dryly, coming over with the cup of coffee. "You make terrible coffee."

"I concentrate on the finer things of life." She picked up her suitcase. Stuart took it from her and carried it down on the escalator. He had a car waiting with a chauffeur that looked like he came off a nineteenth-century waterfront.

But at the front door stood Stanley Rauch with a gun pointed at Sibyl. "Sorry," he said. "Did you plan to go somewhere?"

CHAPTER V

"Just for a little visit to my home," Stuart explained.

"With a suitcase?"

"She doesn't really need the suitcase."

"Yes. You can have it," Sibyl said, handing the grip to Stanley.

Stanley looked unhappy. "I think we better check in at headquarters. I'm sorry, Sergeant Blue, but the chief was afraid you'd try a skip. He thinks you have a way of finding out things about Centaurians before he does."

"I do."

Sibyl glanced at Stuart and Stuart glanced at his chauffeur, who made a quiet leap out of the car and removed Stanley's gun and knocked him out silently, all in one smooth gesture.

"Let's not stand here and watch your bridges burning," Stuart said. He handed Sibyl into the handsome, black Dalmation. "Home base, Hatty," he told the chauffeur, "and don't meander."

The Dalmation shot off like a bullet.

"Those are your bridges burning, too, you know," Sibyl said. "This is the first thing we've had to pin on you."

"We?" Stuart grinned.

"They." Surely this wasn't she, Sibyl Sue Blue, on the wrong side of the law! Sibyl wiped her hand over her forehead. How had all this happened? Things had gone so fast and there had been no time to explain things to Lieutenant Brandt or Stanley because Stuart had been there, listening. And poor Stanley...

There was the sound of a police siren in the distance. "Don't worry so much," Stuart said. "That siren's not for us."

"I wasn't worried. I was thinking."

"About what?" He took her hand, and whatever she had been thinking about deserted her. She thought she could feel his whole body, the pulsing of his blood, the slidings of his muscles, in the hand around hers.

Hatty got them out of the city by a side route and finally Sibyl recognized the single-lane road where Dr. Beadle had come, on that wild ride through the rain.

The structure that loomed behind the barn turned out to be a deserted-looking Victorian mansion, with flapping, long unpainted gingerbread and crazy turrets that stared blackly out of shattered windows. A rooster weather vane, slightly off balance, spun in the wind.

Sibyl got out into a hot sun and cold wind, feeling very unreal. There was a surge of cricket noises and then a silence, as when the creatures of the grass listen.

Sibyl laughed a little. "I feel as though I've dropped into a hole in time," she said. "A hundred and fifty years ago."

"We'll accelerate a hundred years when we go inside," Stuart said. "You wait out here, Hatty. Let Beadle in when he comes."

Stuart brought Sibyl through the barn, out again on the other side, into the back door of the mansion, through a little door, and then he did something to a wall of steel behind the door and it slid open.

"I see what you mean about the hundred years ahead," Sibyl said. "It looks like the Satellite Homes architects and engineers keep designing. I fondly assume that is not a pillar of fire over there?"

Stuart laughed. "It's an armchair. Go sit in it and see."

The "chair" fitted itself comfortably around Sibyl and adjusted itself to her body temperature. Then it murmured, "You weigh a hundred and five pounds today." Sibyl laughed, looked for the door and saw it had closed seamlessly behind them.

"Is this where you live?" Sibyl asked.

"No. I've got a deluxe mansion in town where my wife keeps her bourbon. This is just my little hideaway. Like it?"

"Not bad. Is that a bar you're pulling out from the wall?"

"It is." Stuart mixed Sibyl a gin and 'gin. "I've ordered breakfast," he said, handing her the drink and mixing bourbon and lemon for himself.

She drank fast, sucked at her teeth a moment, and gave him a long look. "I wonder how clever you are."

"My mama always thought I was the cleverest little thing that ever was."

"It would be very clever to turn the Centaurians against me, so I can't do any investigating, and turn the police against me so they won't believe me if I do. And to have me cut off the force just when I've produced proof that Radix viruses are behind the murders."

"It was your idea to come with me on this jaunt."

"I don't have much choice now, do I? And I don't dare even call Missy."

"If you haven't murdered any Centaurians, why don't you go back and defend yourself?" Was there a mocking look in his eye or not?

"I might," Sibyl said. "Would you let me out of that door?"

"Try it."

Did he know she wouldn't, couldn't now?

"Never mind. Only if you decide not to take me with you after all, I'll be... irritated."

A chrome table laid with breakfast wheeled itself forward through some invisible door. Sibyl could have eaten both plates, but she restrained herself from snatching at Stuart's scrambled eggs.

It had been a long time since she'd sat across breakfast with a man, and she had to keep reminding herself, through the faintly domestic glow of it all, that this was a dangerous man. Subtle, clever, secretive. And as yet she hadn't the faintest glimmer what he was really like.

Some people reveal themselves so completely that you can find their whole character in their smallest gesture. Stuart Grant wasn't one of those.

Something buzzed and Stuart thumbed on the telephone and pressed the button into his ear. He laughed and cut off.

"The police are searching the house," he said. "This apartment cost in the neighborhood of fifty thousand dollars, and unless you measure up with a micrometer, you can't guess it's here. Depends on which way you come in that door." Stuart poured her a cup of coffee from a hiccupping percolator.

"You make coffee worse than me," Sibyl remarked.

"I concentrate on the finer things." He grinned evilly. "There's the door opening. It's Beadle, no doubt. Hello, Beadle. I hope you're your usual rollicking self this morning."

Dr. Beadle frowned. "National Lead is down one quarter this morning." He had his black bag with him. He looked at the breakfast dishes and then at Sibyl. "You ate?" he asked accusingly.

"Of course I ate. Why not?"

He sighed. "How am I going to do the blood sugar? Oh, well. I'll do what I can with a gross examination. I've got your record from last year from the Schenthal computer. A woman your age ought to go through every six months."

Stuart laughed. "I'll get things organized for take-off while you do all that with the needles. Let me know if she has Oriental botulism."

"There is no such disease," Dr. Beadle said seriously.

"I gather I'm going to have to have a medical examination," Sibyl said.

"Naturally," Stuart answered. "You don't just hop on a spaceship and take off. You have to be examined, cleaned, sprayed, vaccinated, inoculated, educated, excavated, pollinated..." He went out and the door slid closed behind him.

"All right, Dr. Beadle," Sibyl said as he fitted on his stethoscope, "I want to finish the conversation we started the other evening. Do you know why I was under attack by green Centaurians? After all, you discovered chlorosis."

"Cough," said Dr. Beadle. "No. I didn't know about these attacks. Do you often feel persecuted, Mrs. Blue?"

"Only when I'm attacked. Stuart says he doesn't know anything about it, either. But whenever a chlorotic Centaurian sees me, he reacts immediately by wanting to kill me."

There was a pause while Dr. Beadle listened to Sibyl's heart in different places. He frowned.

"Something wrong with my heart?" Sibyl asked anxiously.

"No. I was just thinking about National Lead again. Please jump up and down on your right foot twenty-five times."

"Then there must be some agency at work that you and Stuart ought to know about. Some plot... or counterplot. Oh, all right. One, two, three, four, five..."

"It is possible, from what you've told me about your own reaction and immunity," Dr. Beadle said slowly, "that these attacks on you personally, and no one else, are an effect of the virus on the chlorotic brain. An antivirus to your husband's protective virus, so to speak."

"Twenty-*five*," Sibyl said. "I don't understand."

"Your husband sent you a message and also a virus to protect you against the effects of the Radix virus. So that whatever it was originally supposed to do, it would do *to you*. Now, the virus thus under attack might cause the infected person—a Centaurian with chlorosis—to see you, and only you, as an enemy. Please lie down on the sofa."

The plastic sofa was cold and so were Dr. Beadle's hands. To what extent was this irritating little man a murderer? "Can you tell me," she asked, "how long these suicides are going to go on after we leave for Radix? Isn't there some way to stop them?"

"Please sit up and cross your right knee over your left. I am unable to answer your question, except to say that there are probably only a few, if any, of the Radix cigarettes left, which a private investigation has not located. When and if they are used up, the... um, disease... will cease. I am going to take some of your blood now, to make a serum."

"For what?"

"A specific antivirus for Radix. It will be safer to have it along. I've been... that is... the encapsulated human livers were saved for a purpose. I rather feel—oh, never mind."

"Now that you've got my blood," Sibyl said with a sudden terrible suspicion, "I hope this doesn't mean I get thrown out on the garbage heap!"

"No. Why?" Dr. Beadle asked.

"I don't know," Sibyl said. "I'm asking."

"Then is there anything you know about Radix? About what's there? I don't mean your dream."

Sibyl smoothed down her hair, adjusted her skirt. "You mean has Stuart told me anything? No." She gave Dr. Beadle a searching look. He was fitting a capsule into another needle. "There's a lot you don't know, isn't there? And you're a little afraid, aren't you?"

Dr. Beadle plunged the needle into her arm. "If you have a reaction to this, take three aspirin tablets with a glass of milk."

When Dr. Beadle left, Sibyl sat down, lit a cigar, and thought about the Radix-benzale cigarettes that might be left on Centaurus or on Earth. She thought about Missy and Jimmy and... she had to talk to Brandt. No use trying the telephone. It would be monitored.

She slid the door back, pressing where Dr. Beadle had pressed, and walked through the old barn and out into a sunshine so brilliant it made her eyes hurt for a moment. The Dalmation was parked in the drive and Hatty was walking up and down, swinging the keys.

"Hello," said Stuart, coming up behind her and making her jump. "Dr. Beadle tells me you have a good heart."

"Yes, you lucky boy. You know, you could use a little landscaping around here." The weeds grew high and the only cheery thing in sight was a little clump of blackeyed Susans bobbing like laughter in the breeze.

"I like weeds," Stuart said. "Are you about ready for lunch?"

Sibyl was timing Hatty's walk. She counted his steps again. "In a moment," she said. "Oh, I left my cigars in your hide-out. Could you...?"

Stuart looked at her suspiciously. "You aren't thinking of making off, are you? This is no time to change your mind. The ship is revving up and take-off is in four hours."

Sibyl watched for her moment. She counted, tripped Stuart quickly so he went down flat on the flagstone steps, leaped to Hatty and chopped deftly at his key hand with the side of her hand, threw him quickly over her shoulder, rammed the key into the ignition of the heavy Dalmation, and screeched off.

She tore around in a circle on two wheels and sped down the narrow lane, took a left onto a wider road when she came to it, went on to the leafless sycamore. She got out onto the highway in less than ten minutes and wove in and out of leisurely midday traffic into the city and careened around side streets to the station.

Stanley sat in the visitor's chair in Brandt's office, giving a report, and he rose to his feet in shock and rage when Sibyl came in, slammed the door behind her and stood against it, catching her breath. Stanley had a bandage on his head.

Brandt regarded her calmly. "Glad you've decided to come back and face it, Sibyl," he said. "You can't spend the rest of your life running, even if you've got Stuart Grant to run with."

"I'll explain it," she said, with a glance at Stanley's furious face. "But I haven't finished my investigation. Sorry, Stanley, but I was in a hurry. First, am I still on the force?"

"Technically, yes," Brandt said. He switched on the tape recorder.

Sibyl began to talk, fast but clearly. She hadn't had time to think it all out before hand, but now everything seemed to click into place as she spoke.

"Here's the picture as I see it. Ten years ago the first expedition went to Radix and was captured by an intelligent life form. Last year, Stuart Grant led a second expedition to Radix and obtained a virus from this life form which was to change Centaurians in some way. Perhaps change them into Radix-type life forms. I don't know for what purpose. Perhaps some agreement with the Radix intelligence.

"But the virus which was to accomplish these things didn't work right. Stuart distributed the virus indiscriminately, via benzale cigarettes, and all it did was cause chlorosis in Centaurians. But, whether by Grant's plan or not, some of these cigarettes were brought to Earth along with regular benzale cigarettes. In human beings, the virus had a more violent effect, influencing the mind and finally encapsulating in the liver. See my report for that.

"Dr. Wilfred T. Beadle, hired by Stuart Grant, then began to collect this virus after it had encapsulated in the liver and the victim—dying of liver dysfunction—had removed it from his or her own body. Bella Kale walked into that schoolroom alone after removing her own liver. Technically, I suppose, Bella Kale committed suicide. But the big question is set up now and it's got to be answered." Sibyl sat down and tried to catch her breath. She felt as though she hadn't breathed since she counted Hatty's steps and poised to chop the keys out of his hand.

"Big question," Lieutenant Brandt echoed. "So far you haven't offered any proof at all about who's guilty of what. I don't quite see what you're getting at."

"I know. The part about what might have happened on Radix is pure guesswork. There might not be an intelligent life form there at all. Though it must at least be biologically highly organized. But let me finish. Along with the Radix virus, my husband managed to send a message and a... protective virus, I suppose, which he hoped in some way would reach me. It was a hope not entirely wild, since I live in a port city and work for the police. This made my blood a carrier of antivirus, which cured Gracia Joad, and Stanley had better get Doc immediately to take some of my blood and make a proper serum from it. Dr. Mason took some, but he said he wasn't prepared to do it the right way."

Stanley got up and went out. If he thought this was a lot of foolishness he didn't say so.

"Stuart Grant," Sibyl went on, "is about to take off for Radix again and I talked to Beadle and he says some more of these cigarettes may be around. Stay alert for Centaurians with faintly greenish scales and for people with symptoms of Radix poisoning. The first thing they try to do is hide. All this is in the report I made night before last, when we brought Gracia Joad in. Do you have a cigar? I came off without my purse."

Lieutenant Brandt pulled out his box of guest cigars and offered one to Sibyl. He lit it with the guest lighter on his desk. Somehow, more than anything else, this made Sibyl feel that suddenly her role was reversed. She was on the outside of the police force. The hunted, not the hunter.

"The big question," Sibyl went on, "is why that virus was brought to Centaurus and then to Earth. If we don't find out, the specter of Radix will always be there to haunt us. Who or what might come later to threaten the Earth?"

Doc came in and Sibyl rolled up her sleeve while he rummaged among his instruments. "Any objections if I take a whole pint? I wish you were bigger."

"I wish I were bigger, too," Sibyl said. "But take a good swig."

Lieutenant Brandt shook his head as if to clear it. "I hope you know how unbelievable all this sounds. Menace from Outer Space! Why don't we concentrate on Wilfred T. Beadle for the moment? Is he at Stuart's hide-out?"

Sibyl left that one. "I don't have much time. Stuart Grant is going to Radix and I want to go with him and see this thing through."

Brandt made an impatient noise through his teeth. "Let's suppose for a moment that I'm willing to incur Centaurian criticism and that

I don't mind being made a fool of. Suppose I believe everything you say. Then how do I know that your husband, on Radix, isn't the Menace from Outer Space?"

Sibyl stood perfectly still and let the thought spread through her and disappear. "I never thought of that," she said. "Not for a moment. It isn't possible."

"Then let me throw out another possibility. Suppose instead of being an officer of the law on the trail of a criminal, you are a highly emotional woman in love with Stuart Grant?"

Sibyl dislodged a lovely ash from the end of her cigar.

"You think the two things have to be exclusive?" she asked softly.

Brandt made a face. "Women detectives! All right. It isn't easy for me, but I'm going to let you go because I don't think anything, even death, would hurt you more than not going." He stood up and held out a hand. "Good luck, Sergeant."

Sibyl shook the hand, and then took Stanley's. "Thank you." And ran out quickly, both because she was in a hurry and because she didn't want to spoil things by crying.

Back through the quiet afternoon streets she drove, thinking of how many threads she was leaving dangling, going off like this. No proper good-byes to Missy, people left with no explanation — Llanr; even Jimmy; the Carters, who were supposed to come for dinner Saturday night — the utilities still on in her apartment, the telephone still answering without her. Messages to no one.

It was like sudden death. But, Sibyl thought, coming to the end of the narrow road and seeing Hatty pacing the weedy walk in front of Stuart's barn, the world will close over the space I leave, and it won't matter.

Hatty came up and stuck his hand through the window. "Look," he said. "Look what you done to me. I gotta bruise. My shootin' hand!"

"Sorry, Hatty. But if I'd asked permission to use the car, you'd have said no, now wouldn't you?"

"I ain't the boss. Mr. Grant is. And it's a good thing you come back with this car. He needs it."

Stuart appeared as Sibyl was slamming the car door behind her.

"You came back alone?" he asked, surprised.

"Of course. What did you expect?"

"A squad of police cars. Why did you run away?"

"I didn't want to leave without saying good-bye."

"Sentiment!" Stuart made a face. "I don't have time to do anything about this except leave. Get back in the car." He reached in and honked the horn three times. Four men came out, got in the back seat. "Move over," Stuart said, pushing Sibyl aside, getting into the driver's seat himself while Hatty got in next to Sibyl. Stuart ran the car in a series of smooth motions, as though it were a part of his autonomic nervous system.

"Gut," he said over his shoulder at one of the men, "may I ask why you have a gun pointed at Joe Rabinsky?" Joe was a small, narrow-chested man, and he had that sort of anxious, honest eyes that are almost painful to see.

"I don't want to go, Mr. Grant," Joe answered, cutting in on Gut before he could answer. "I changed my mind, because I just found out my wife's going to have a baby, and we might not be back in time."

"I thought you weren't married," Stuart said. "You weren't supposed to be married."

"I wasn't, sir. But I couldn't let my wife have a baby without being married to her, could I?"

"You couldn't... never mind. I'm sorry, Joe, but it's too late to change your mind. You're a good navigator and we need you."

"But, sir, you got no legal right to have this man point a gun at me. This ain't the army, and if I want to change my mind..."

"You'd better find out right now that I don't worry about what I have a right to do. On the *Albatross* my word is law. There isn't any democracy."

"Where are we going?" Sibyl asked.

Stuart looked around at her and laughed. "To Radix."

"Now?"

"Now."

And the thing that worried Sibyl all the way to the landing strip, where Stuart's great ships came and went, was that she didn't have her purse. Her social security card, the rest of her cigars, her picture of Missy, her rouge stick, her comb.

Suddenly Sibyl's emotions all sprang out at her at once—the un-shed tears for her friends, the worry about Missy that she hid so care-fully from herself, the little man with the gun pointed at him and his sad little wife somewhere, the strangeness of what she was going into. She burst into tears.

"What's the matter?" Stuart asked.

"I forgot my comb," she explained, and sobbed quietly.

CHAPTER VI

It was a monstrous silver bullet, pouring out smoke, poised on its trestle. It was as big as the Centaurus-bound cargo ships around it. It was windowless, like a coffin.

"Scared?" Stuart said at her with a grin.

"No," Sibyl answered truthfully. "Just excited. I wish it had windows."

"It has. In the lounge and in the navigation room. We'll slide the steel back later. And I'll find you a comb as soon as we settle in," he added.

Hatty opened the door and handed them out of the car, wincing as he used his bruised hand. "Boss," he said, "we didn't prepare no accommodation for the lady."

"I forgot to tell you," Stuart said. "She can stay with me. She'll make a good bodyguard."

Hatty's face fell. "Gee, Boss, I'm sorry I fell down on the job. I wasn't watching and she was fast and anyhow you don't expect no lady to make no brutal attack like that." He glowered at Sibyl.

Stuart refrained from laughing. "I didn't mean that, Hatty. You're my bodyguard still. We're taking Sergeant Blue here along as a... mascot." He patted Sibyl on the head.

"I'd wag my tail," Sibyl said, "if there weren't so many people around." She followed Stuart up the ramp, through the lock and into a maze of hallways and rooms that she knew would be soon as familiar to her as her apartment at home. There was a fairly large lounge with a bar, like a hotel lounge. There was the control room, with its tiers of dials and instruments, and Joe stopped there and started adjusting switches while she and Stuart went on. There was an efficient chrome

71

kitchen, which looked much too sophisticated to have food in it, and a series of surprisingly graceful little dining rooms.

"There's so much of it," Sibyl observed, "Just to take Stuart Grant to Radix. It makes me think of Victorian estates, with hordes of servants and one little bitty old man to be taken care of."

"I'm not a little bitty old man. And the reason for all the space is that this is one of my Centaurus line ships. It's cheaper to use it than it would be to build a smaller one just for the Radix trip."

"Then you don't plan a lot of trips. Where does that impressive-looking door lead to?"

Stuart smiled. "Open it. It's the best view in the ship. Just don't ever open it after we take off."

Sibyl opened the door and then stepped back quickly. The door opened into a vast, black, empty space.

"That's the explosion chamber," Stuart explained.

"You should have given me a little gold key to it," Sibyl said. "And told me I could enter any room on the ship except just that one. Then one day when you were out hunting I would have been overcome by curiosity and blam! You see, I would have been sure the room was full of ex-wives on hooks."

"I don't have any ex-wives. Just that one you saw at the bar of the Stilton. She's always switching careers. She used to be a nymphomaniac. Now she's an alcoholic. She doesn't love me any more and she keeps trying to divorce me, but she can't stay sober long enough."

"Why don't you divorce her?"

"I like having a wife. It keeps other women from being able to marry me."

"And where does *that* door lead?"

"That's the one I'll give you the little gold key for."

"No, really, where does it go?"

"That's the cargo hold." He gave her an odd look.

"And what's in it?"

"It really doesn't matter."

Sibyl leaned close to the door and frowned. She thought she heard curious noises — a dragging and clinking sound.

And was that something like a muffled scream? Heavy things sliding or bumping?

But Stuart turned her around and took her face in his hands, look-ing into her eyes. "We've got more important things to think about," he said.

And she thought wildly, he's going to kiss me. But he didn't. She was glad for a moment and then annoyed.

She followed him up a ramp and through a door that said *Stuart Grant* into a luxurious cabin. The room contained a large, rather or-nate bed, a carved desk with a tape reader on it, and a shelf of tapes above. There was also a minute washbasin and a glassed-off shower stall. And a closet full of Stuart's clothes.

"Hatty will bring your things in a minute," Stuart said.

"What things?"

"There are various female accouterments in the ship's stores. If they don't fit, I expect you're handy with a needle."

"I am not. Where do *I* sleep? On the floor?"

"If you like. In about half an hour you'll hear a siren. That means take-off. You lie down. Flat. We don't take off at three G but it's still uncomfortable, especially if you're not used to it."

"Where are you going now?"

"You sound like my wife. I'm going to supervise a few things."

"Can I get something to eat? I'm starving. I don't even remember when I ate last."

"After take-off. It's better on an empty stomach, anyway."

Hatty came in, looking surly, with an armful of dresses packaged in plastic and a box of assorted make-up. Sibyl picked out a couple of wrap-around dresses she could tie to fit, though they were just a bit long. She breathed a sigh of relief over the cold cream. Two months or more without cold cream would have ruined her skin forever. She picked out a rouge stick that wasn't too far off for her coloring. There was no jewelry, no perfume. But there was a good, split-toothed comb and a hard brush.

Sibyl took a quick shower, put on clean clothes and make-up. And finished just in time for the warning whistle.

"I'm still starving." Sibyl said when Stuart came in. She was sitting at Stuart's desk, trying to think what could have been making those noises — if they were noises — in the cargo hold. But she found she couldn't really think about anything except food and Stuart Grant. And remembered how when she was a teen-ager she always used to think she was in love before dinner, and found out after a good meal that really she'd only been hungry.

"Starving," Stuart echoed, his mind still occupied with whatever he'd just been doing—what *was* he thinking about? "Oh, yes." And Sibyl sensed him now concentrating on her. And it was suddenly as though he never thought about anything on earth except Sibyl Sue Blue. "Yes. Let's have a drink and dinner in the lounge."

Sibyl followed Stuart down the hall, wishing she had something besides a plain wrap-around to wear. At least earrings, or a nice pin. The door of the lounge slid open at Stuart's approach. It was large and deserted-looking, but Stuart led her to a comer that was cozy and softly lit.

"Steak and Spanish?" he asked, pushing buttons. "Yes, rare," he said into the intercom. "I don't like waiters," he added to Sibyl. "They distract me."

He pulled out a bar from a fluorescent-lit plant stand, and handed Sibyl a bowl of crackers and mixed her a gin and 'gin. She took a sip, sighed, and wished there were a button to push so as to stop time in its tracks. So Stuart would always be unknown but about-to-be known to her, so the ship would never get to Radix.

"When are you going to tell me why you're going to Radix?" she asked. "And what you intend to bring back?"

"Bring back? Verdant ideas," he said unexpectedly. "Can't you concede me scientific curiosity?"

"I could," Sibyl said, "if I didn't suspect you of being a murderer."

Stuart rattled the ice in his glass and looked to see what kind of fortune it told. "You've got nice knees," he said. "Just these odd mental difficulties. Who was murdered?"

"Well, suicides, then."

Stuart caught her eyes with his and held them. "Would you believe me," he said slowly, "if I told you I had nothing to do with that? And that I was searching like mad for a way to prevent them?"

"Then you brought the virus back by accident?"

A gorgeous pair of steaks wheeled themselves in on a steel table.

Sibyl finished her drink and eyed them hungrily.

"Look," Stuart said, "let's go into this sometime when we know each other better. When you can understand it all."

"That's just it," Sibyl said, cutting her steak. "Oh, I can't talk with my mouth watering like this." She lit into the steak ungracefully, and when she stopped being so ravenously hungry, she looked up at Stuart. He smiled his handsome smile and the curl sprawled over his forehead. He was amused, watching her eat. He, too, was eating, but in a businesslike way. He didn't seem to much enjoy it, any more than he took real pleasure in drinking.

Sibyl noted this, still trying to sort him out, to have him come forth in her mind as a person she could understand, predict. What was he like with sex? Did he sort of push it about on his plate, too?

"You," she said finally. "What are you like, Stuart Grant?"

He burst into laughter. "What a question! Well—you can hear the story of my life, if you don't already know it. I've always been rich. I had a gold-plated crib and the handle of my pacifier was set with diamonds. My mother adored me so much she refused to have any more children. My father spent all his time making money—but I didn't really appreciate that until I grew up."

Sibyl looked around for a cigar, but of course no smoking was allowed. She didn't want one, because Dr. Beadle had included some antismoking drug in her shots. But she wanted to want one and was annoyed. "Which one did you hate?" she asked.

"My mother," he answered. "For poking at me all me all the time. I ran away when I was sixteen, hid on a freighter to Centaurus—one of my father's freighters—and worked for a year as a valet to the chief of a little-known tribe of Middle Island Centaurians in the northern sector."

"I didn't know all that," Sibyl said.

"My disappearance was kept quiet. By the time I was seventeen I was grown up. I came back to Earth, went on to college and took degrees in engineering, chemistry and linguistics."

"And became a business administrator."

"Yes. Along the way I married a beautiful, vapid girl who adored me."

"Like your mother."

"I suppose so. She, too, poked at me all the time, until I finally took to just ignoring her. That's the one thing that'll make a woman give up."

"And of course you supply her with a good grade of bourbon so you needn't feel guilty about her."

"Guilty!" Stuart cried. "It isn't my fault she's a nuisance."

"No children?" It was impossible to picture Stuart as a father.

"Her! A mother!" Stuart gave an odd laugh. "No. I might have... now I have other plans."

Sibyl shook her head. "You haven't *really* told me about yourself. You've got youth, looks, money, freedom — what is it you want besides?"

"At the moment," Stuart said, "I want to improve my friendship with you. Have you stopped to consider that we've known each other all this time and we've hardly even held hands?"

Sibyl felt the good steak in her stomach, relaxing her and spreading a feeling of well-being throughout her body. She ought to be frightened, lonely, insecure, frozen with worry about Missy and the future.

"If that bar has a hi-fi set, why don't we turn it on and let's dance," she shrugged. "I feel as though I know people better when I've danced with them."

Stuart did something to a switch and the lights glowed off and the music on. Familiar moonlight music, but played with an odd, serpentine rhythm. Stuart took her in his arms and guided her into a sinuous dance step. He danced as he drove a car, with assurance and power, so that he was easy to follow. Sibyl wanted to ask him where he learned to dance like that, but it was a moment too tight with other meanings to be ruined by talking.

She closed her eyes and followed him into the eerie longings of the music.

The next morning Sibyl waked up to find herself helplessly in love with Stuart. She reached for him but there was only the warm, crumpled place in the bed where he had been. She rolled over to his side and rubbed her face in his pillow. It was a horrible, consuming love, as she'd known it would be. All night she'd been wrapped in it, slept in it. And yet—yet in her dreams there had still been gliding green images, vegetable thoughts and the voice of Kenneth calling through green aisles and always forever distant.

And sometimes she'd waked confusedly, thinking of Missy. But it was hopeless to think of Missy. All Sibyl could do was hope that what she'd already done for Missy was right, or at least not wrong.

She got up, feeling a little groggy and unreal, as though she'd been drunk the night before. But she hadn't been. She remembered every detail.

She washed, dressed, wandered out into the halls. Where was Stuart? Where did he go when he wasn't with her? The ship seemed so empty, though Sibyl knew there was a crew of forty. Forty-one counting herself.

Hatty came busily by, looking uncomfortable in a merchant space uniform that was much too trim for his hulk. He bobbed his head at Sibyl, stood in a doorway so she could pass.

"Have you seen Mr. Grant?" Sibyl asked.

"Yes'm. He's with the... he's busy."

"With the *what*?"

"The cargo." Hatty glared at Sibyl. He obviously didn't know how much she knew.

"What cargo?"

"Just cargo," Hatty said. "Mr. Grant don't confide in nobody. You stick to being a lady friend and let Mr. Grant run the ship."

Sibyl went on by, up to the lounge, and gasped. Because the steel shutters had been retracted and beyond the glassplex was the brilliant spread of still stars in a black sky. Dr. Beadle was looking at it rather irritably, as though it were not quite what it ought to be.

Sibyl laughed—it was so typical—and he jumped.

"What's wrong with the sky?" she asked.

"Nothing. I've been in space before. But I lose the feeling of motion. And all that out there looks like a fake. Tell me, Mrs. Blue, do you... what plans do you have for when we get to Radix?"

"Plans! How could I have any plans when I don't know what's going to happen? Don't even know what it looks like!"

"I thought perhaps Mr. Grant might have discussed it with you."

"We had other topics of conversation," Sibyl said demurely.

"Look, Dr. Beadle, you don't like me and I don't like you. But why don't we compare notes and see if we can figure out what Radix is like?"

"Because," Dr. Beadle said, walking toward the door, "I don't know any more than you do about it. And you don't know any more than I, unless Mr. Grant has told you something."

"How do you know that?"

He almost smiled. "I just know."

Sibyl though about the benzale cigarette he'd given her, and that she'd smoked. Had she then talked in her sleep? But he had gone before the cigarette took effect. Then why had she waked up remembering his voice?

"Then tell me," Sibyl said. "What is the cargo?"

"Ask Mr. Grant." And he let the door to the lounge slide quietly closed behind him.

Sibyl stared out at the endless, star-hung night.

She couldn't find Stuart. She passed the door that led to the hold and pressed her ear against it and heard only faint noise or vibration that might have been the ship's motors.

The little gold key. But which one was it? And how could she get hold of it, since he either kept his keys on him or under his pillow at night? Sibyl went back to Stuart's cabin. His desk drawer was locked. Another little gold key. She'd like to have a look at the black notebook he'd put in there.

Instead, she experimented with a safety pin on the shoulder of her wrap-around dress until she got a fairly chic little set of gathers, and then explored until she found the dining rooms and a crewman willing to bring her breakfast.

The rest of the day she spent exploring the ship, hoping for at least a glimpse of Stuart.

Then, that night—Earth time—Stuart appeared as she was dressing for dinner, putting on a fresh wrap-around dress and pinning it into a semblance of a ruche at the neck. He came in and said, almost domestically, "Well, what have you been doing all day?"

"Nothing," she answered truthfully, and was about to ask him the same question and realized she was so hopeless about him that she couldn't run the slightest risk of annoying him. Suppose he thought she was poking at him, and suppose he should turn on his heel and ignore her for the rest of the trip?

"Nothing," she repeated. "Is... is everything going well for you?"

Stuart grinned broadly. "That's the way I like you, baby."

And so the days wore on and Sibyl tried uselessly to reason with herself, to clear her mind, to think of Kenneth and Missy and why she was going to Radix and what she ought to be doing...

Even so. Even in the thick fog of her love for Stuart, Sibyl remembered, as though it were her job some other place, some other time, that she was still trying to find out what was behind the benzale murders. And still, as her green dreams came and went, she held a wild hope that somewhere, somehow, Kenneth was not dead. And she knew that she could sacrifice Stuart for Kenneth if only she could find him.

And though she found her whole being occupied with the smallest things about Stuart—the way the small hair grew on his hands, the movement of his eyelids as he spoke, the timbres of his voice heard unexpectedly—even so she kept a small reasonable part of herself, out of sheer pride, and she tried to find out what she could about what was ahead on Radix.

Stuart as yet would tell her nothing. Not what function she was expected to serve, not what Radix was like, not what cargo was in the hold. So she decided to find out what she could from some of the crew members. Maybe they knew something and maybe they didn't. But soon they'd be at Radix, and Sibyl would have to prepare herself as best she could.

She walked along the narrow halls, and by the enormous windows of the lounge she saw a familiar figure, little Joe, staring out at the black immensities of space, looking glum in every muscle.

"Anyway, you got a chance to marry her before you left," Sibyl said.

"Yeah. I hope she knows to get my money out of the bank and all," Joe said. "She ain't too bright. Good-hearted, but not smart in brains, if you know what I mean."

"You'll go back. Surely she can get by for a couple more months."

Joe looked out at the implacable darkness again. "I hope."

"What does that mean?"

"You don't know nothing? Living with Mr. Grant, if you'll excuse the expression."

Sibyl grinned. "He doesn't tell me anything at all."

"Well, it's just scuttlebutt, but it has me worried. There's plenty supplies to get to Radix. But there ain't plenty to get back. In fact, there ain't near enough to get back. It's what they say in the galley. It makes you think, if you know what I mean."

"Oh, surely that's a mistake. I mean there are probably more supplies in the cargo hold or somewhere."

Joe sighed, ran his hands through his overgrown crop of black hair. "I wouldn't like to tell you the rumors about what's in the cargo hold, ma'am."

"But don't you see, Mr. Grant certainly doesn't plan to stay on Radix the rest of his life, and he has to have supplies to come back. If Radix were a civilized planet, with people on it, then maybe I could see it. But I assure you, Mr. Grant doesn't plan to spend the rest of his life admixing the plants on Radix."

"Well, he wouldn't be planning to start a colony, would he, ma'am?"

"With no women?"

"Well, there's you, if you'll excuse me."

Sibyl frowned to herself. One woman age forty who already had hot flashes now and then? "Hardly."

"Then," Joe went on, "maybe he's going to make monsters with those 'things' down there in the hold."

"What 'things'?"

"Rumors, Miss. Don't nobody but Mr. Grant and Hatty and Dr. Beadle go down there, but we hear noises, sometimes. Like heavy things moving. Talking. Groaning. Hatty and the doctor, they ain't conversational, if you know what I mean."

"You're thinking about Frankenstein's monster? No, I can't see Stuart doing that, either."

"Then why do you think he's doing this? Going to Radix at all? You know what it costs, fueling a ship like this, bribing all of us to go?"

"Haven't you talked to anyone that was on the previous trip with Stuart? Can't they tell you anything?"

"That's another thing I found out. There ain't nobody from the trip before. Not on the ship now. Whoever they were, they didn't want to go back. And they kept mighty quiet about Radix, too, because nobody knows nothing. Probably bribed them, too. Don't you know what Radix is like, ma'am? What Mr. Grant wants from it?"

Sibyl sighed. "Ah, if only I knew what Stuart Grant wants, then I think it might all come clear." But how could she know what he wanted, what motivated him, what he was really like? As long as she was in love with him, she wasn't capable of knowing anything about him. She couldn't even remember how he had seemed to her before she fell in love with him. And she could find no way not to be in love with him.

Still, she forced herself to watch him, and one night, being so sure of her, he grew careless and left his keys out on the desk. Sibyl waited, in the quiet darkness of the cabin, with a scented breeze blowing from the air conditioner, until she heard the deep, even breathing that meant Stuart was in deep sleep. He always slept the quiet sleep of the innocent.

She held her breath, legged carefully over Stuart, tied on a wraparound dress, pressed her hand carefully around the keys so they wouldn't clink when she picked them up, slid the cabin door open and then closed it silently behind her. And prayed the moment of light it had let into the cabin hadn't waked Stuart.

The hallway was deserted and Sibyl tiptoed along, past Dr. Beadle's cabin, past the lounge and down the stairs. She heard someone pacing slowly along the hall where the door to the cargo hold was. She peered around the edge of the gangway. It was Hatty.

She waited for him to pace back close to her, watched him bring his hand to his mouth to stifle a yawn, and then darted out and clipped him behind the ear, caught him and let him down gently, face first so if he suddenly regained consciousness he wouldn't see her. She ripped off his shirt, and quickly bound and gagged him, blindfolded him, and rolled him into the nearest cabin. He'd be able to get himself untied, but it would take time.

Sibyl paused a moment as she started to press the key against the door to the cargo hold. She didn't have a weapon of any kind on her. There might be any kind of thing down there. Hungry lions. What if…

She slid the door back, felt for the light switch within, because it was pitch dark. And almost fell down the gangway. Chained to the deck, hands and feet also chained together, were four Centaurians. And the biggest one was Rrinn, whose teeth she had cracked on the sidewalk in front of the C house, whose lighted Radix cigarette she had stolen. All the Centaurians were fast asleep.

She closed the door behind her, went down the gangway and bent over Rrinn. His heavy jowls sagged to one side in his sleep, and now his greenish coloration was gone. There was a heavy chain that made a dent in his fat thigh.

She shook his shoulder and shouted, "Rrinn!" In as loud a whisper as she dared. He stirred and she shook him again. Slowly his eyelids parted — in the birdlike way of Centaurians — and he looked at her groggily.

"It's *me!*" she hissed. "Sibyl Sue Blue. I clobbered you at the Centaurian party." She shook him again. "Rrinn! What are you doing here?"

"Here," he echoed, and then seemed to come to life. "I don't know. I went to sleep with a beautiful Earth girl one night and when I woke up I was here with these others. In chains. Nobody was around. We shouted and tried to break loose. And then there was the smell of anesthetic in the air — sprayed in through the air conditioner, I think, and… got a cigarette?"

"No. You can't smoke on a spaceship."

"Ship! We're on a ship! That accounts for a lot." He closed his eyes briefly, and then was immediately asleep again.

Sibyl shook him, infuriated. It was too cold down here, and the hum of the air conditioners had an otherworldly whine. She felt lonely, deserted. "Rrinn! Then you don't know why you were kidnapped? You have no idea?"

"No. No idea."

"What about the others? Do they know?"

Rrinn shook his head slowly.

Sibyl dug her nails into his arm, to keep him awake. "But is there anything to tie you and the others together? Anything that—" She looked more closely at one sprawled a little way off from Rrinn. Chlorosis. "Have you all had chlorosis?"

Rrinn had again gone off to sleep. Sibyl got up. There was more she wanted to talk about, but she'd been gone long enough. Too long. She'd found out what was in the cargo hold, anyhow. Hatty would be stirring and would alert the whole ship as soon as he got the gag out of his mouth.

She climbed the gangway, cautiously slid the door back, and looked right into the face of Dr. Beadle, standing there with his black bag in his hand.

"Ssh!" Sibyl said, putting her finger to her lips and running quietly on. She had an idea he wouldn't tell on her. He was worried about what would happen when they got to Radix, depending in some obscure way on Sibyl. Did he simply want an ally, or was it something specific he thought he might need of her? Or perhaps he only wanted the influence he thought she might have with Stuart Grant.

Sibyl was creeping quietly through the cold, dimly lit hallways. She pressed the door to the cabin open, saw the light from the hall briefly light up Stuart as he lay crossways on the bed, and closed the door quickly. He stirred but didn't waken. Sibyl wondered how she could love so much the small sound of his stirring, knowing with her whole body the way the muscles moved under his skin, and still betray him like this.

She carefully felt her way to the desk, picked out the shape of the smallest key, and unlocked the desk drawer. He didn't usually open his desk until after dinner, when he wrote in his black notebook. While Sibyl sat watching the glow of his bent head, pretending to be studying her Centaurian grammar.

"What's that!" Stuart said suddenly, and the bed creaked as he sat up. It was pitch black in the cabin.

"Just me," Sibyl said quickly so that he wouldn't turn on the light. She stripped off her dress and crawled into bed. But Stuart did switch on the light, and looked at her suspiciously, and around the room.

"It was all that beer I had with dinner," Sibyl said. "I tried not to disturb you."

Stuart went over to the desk, picked up his keys, and shook his head at himself. "I left them out, I remember." He tried the desk drawer. "You've been reading my papers!" he said, turning to look accusingly at her.

"In the pitch dark? Oh, darling, what do I care about your papers anyway?" And when he looked at her she really didn't care about the notebook or the Centaurians chained in the cargo hold or anything else.

"I guess you couldn't," he said, satisfied with the look on her face.

But half an hour later when Hatty buzzed him to report he'd been knocked out, Stuart again confronted Sibyl. She burst into tears — real tears, because she couldn't bear it if Stuart found her out.

"All I did was get up and go to the bathroom!" she sobbed. "And you think I knocked out Hatty and read all your papers and next you're going to think I'm poisoning your food. How can you *possibly* think I did all those things?"

"O.K., baby," Stuart said, patting her on the back. "You're right. But there's a traitor on this ship somewhere and I'll find him if I have to tear the crew apart bone by bone. You can help me. You're good at talking to people."

"Oh, yes," Sibyl said. "I want to help. We'll find out."

"You know," Stuart said thoughtfully as he dressed, "I don't trust Beadle. I never know what's he's thinking in that dry little mind of his. But then... what percentage would there be for him in knocking out Hatty? Why —"

"Stuart," Sibyl said, "if you should *choose* to explain all this to me — what's in the cargo hold of the ship and why we're going to Radix — I think I might be able to help a lot better. It's only because I want to... to be all I can to you."

"Yes," Stuart said carefully. "Yes, I think so. Later. Right now I want to question the crew."

When Stuart came back, Sibyl was curled up with a book on Centaurian grammar. She looked up inquiringly.

"Nothing on Hatty's attacker," Stuart said. "If I didn't know Hatty better I'd think it was his imagination."

Sibyl smiled. "Ship still on course?"

Stuart nodded. "Joe's a good navigator, but I check his figures every day. We had to swerve to evade a magnetic storm but we're back on course now. How's your Centaurian coming?"

"O.K.," Sibyl said. "But I'll never learn all those adjectives."

"Don't bother. If they end in *nr* that means they're good, and if they end in *bl* that means they're bad. All the rest of the differences are minor."

"Were you always like that? Even as a child?"

"Like what?"

"Able to grasp essentials immediately. To learn only what is important and not clutter up your mind with exhausting irrelevancies, like the rest of us."

"I could never understand all the things other people worry about, if that's what you mean," Stuart answered.

Sibyl's mind clicked out automatically, Socially Amoral, but she didn't say it. She didn't even think it for very long. Because this man she loved was immune to ordinary laws. That was one of the things that was so wonderful about him.

Sibyl wanted to just sit and watch Stuart. Just watch him while he read or worked with his figures or shaved before lunch or whatever he was going to do.

But what he was going to do was talk. And when he stood over her, smiling oddly, she had no idea what a different person she was going to be within five minutes.

CHAPTER VII

It was then, when the ship was three days out from Radix, that Sibyl fell out of love with Stuart. It was a marvelous feeling.

Perhaps it had been building up in her slowly and she didn't know it. Or perhaps, Sibyl thought, it's some slight shift in hormone balance and someday someone will discover what it is and how to control it and what a lot of trouble *that* will save!

"O.K.," Stuart was saying. "You're about to understand it all now, aren't you, baby?"

Sibyl nodded. Not because she felt she was really about to understand anything, but because Stuart had said that, and whatever he said was true and wonderful.

Looking into his face, Sibyl felt herself, in a split second, possessed by a feeling of tremendous excitement. Something was about to happen to her. Winds puffing out sails in her mind.

"We'll start by letting you look through those notebooks I write in so secretly every night."

It was the look on his face that Sibyl suddenly understood. An assured look. A look of power. He was about to trust her with something. Not because he thought her trustworthy, but because he thought his power over her was complete.

That was the key to Stuart Grant. That was the simple explanation of him. That was his motivation. Power.

That, in turn, was the button to press if you needed to manipulate him.

And suddenly Sibyl didn't love him any more.

She got up quickly, strode trembling to the tiny washbasin and splashed a frugal splash of spaceship water on her face. He mustn't notice.

"I haven't washed my face yet," she explained, implying that she washed it only for him. But he hadn't noticed any difference in her. He was possessed by his feeling of power and he wasn't noticing her. Only his power over her.

She dried her face carefully, smoothing the expression on it. Now she quickly tried to recall to herself how she had felt a few moments before when she was still in love with Stuart, how she had looked.

Stuart opened his desk drawer and Sibyl sat down and picked up the top notebook, the current one, which began with a list of dates and names, starting about three months before. Centaurian names and Centaurian addresses and arrival dates of ships. Further on, Sibyl found names of benzale suicide victims, each numbered, with a date, and a full description of the victim.

"What did you do with the viruses?" Sibyl asked. "The encapsulated human livers?"

"I've got them in a box in the hold."

"Bringing them back to Radix," Sibyl said superfluously, and scanned the pages quickly, stopping short when she came to Rrinn's name and arrival date. "How come Rrinn had instructions to call Dr. Beadle about giving Gracia a Radix cigarette? And if he knew who was getting them, why didn't he stop them?"

"Because," Stuart said, "we had no way of knowing beforehand who was getting them. The instructions gotten to all Centaurians coming in was to call if they found they had *smoked* one. They would know from the reaction. Then we would find out who they had given cigarettes to. Frequently the Radix cigarettes came in batches of two or three together. But by the time we had gotten to the victim, it was too late. If Dr. Beadle had had an antivirus... but he didn't."

Sibyl read on, scanning, and then stopped when she found her own name. There was a full description of her—careful and not very flattering. And later: "Claims husband is Kenneth Blue! How much rapport with Blue? Is she worth fooling with?"

Further on was a full recounting of her benzale dream. Where had he gotten that? And she closed her eyes, being full of the memory of Kenneth, and again heard distantly his voice echoing in her ears.

"I don't understand all of this," Sibyl said. "You have names and dates and formulas and descriptions and lists. But I can't get a clear picture out of it. For instance, the four Centaurian names, including Rrinn's—and it was from him that I got my Radix cigarette—why do you have them listed here separately?"

"That," Stuart said a little smugly, "is what is in the cargo hold."

"The Centaurians!" Sibyl cried, acting as surprised as she could manage to. "But why? Why keep them in the hold? And why bring them to Radix at all? And Stuart... explain it all to me."

"I'll try. I told you once I grew up having everything wanted. I could buy anything—things, people, power. What power you can have in a socialistic world, that is. I went to Radix to see if I could find something new to want. And I did. Sibyl, I found a way to change a world by taking thought. The creative intelligence of Radix permeates in every cell. Every molecule in every cell. So that if you had a Radix plant growing in your garden, and could command it, you could ask it to turn its flowers into rubies, and come back in the morning and pick a king's ransom."

Sibyl closed the notebook with a snap and said, "Darling, it isn't rubies you're after."

"Of course not." Stuart sat down on the edge of the bed, his face alight with excitement. "But think a moment. If you took the Centaurian planet, for instance, and turned Radix loose on it, until all Centaurians were part of a creative intelligence, and if you could direct that intelligence, then you could... 'grasp this Sorry Scheme of Things'—or however it goes—and 'remould it nearer to the Heart's Desire!' "

"Like God," Sibyl murmured.

"Like God," Stuart agreed, with the innocent radiance of obsession. "And furthermore, if you were yourself to become part of Radix, so as to direct from within the creative intelligence, then you would be in effect immortal. You could recreate yourself eternally."

Sibyl stood up, holding the notebook as though it were a firm support. "Yes. I see. But suppose... suppose you were *not* the one who was directing the creative intelligence? Then everything—everyone else—is a slave."

Stuart sighed, put his arms around Sibyl. "You're thinking in obsolete terms, darling. Everyone would be part of the same creative force. You must trust me." He took her chin and raised her face to his.

"You *do* trust me?"

"Of course," Sibyl said.

Stuart was in the lounge with a gun in his hand, questioning the crew one at a time, the next time Sibyl knocked out Hatty. This time she was equipped with a small laser torch which she'd stolen from the supply room. She unlocked the door to the cargo hold, went down the steps and found the four Centaurians awake, eating their dinner as best they could with their hands chained together. No one was with them.

"You may need a fighting chance when we get to Radix," Sibyl explained to Rrinn, going to work on his leg irons with the laser torch, "and I'm doing this to give it to you. But you must not let anyone notice your chains are loosed and you must stay here and not cause any trouble until the ship lands. After that we'll play it by ear and I'll do whatever I can for you."

"But then it may be too late," Rrinn argued. "It would be better to get out now. If you could supply us with weapons we could perhaps take over the ship and turn it back."

Sibyl shook her head, closed one eye and aimed the laser torch away from Rrinn, directly at the chain that held his hands together.

"We're going to land on Radix," she said flatly. "There's a threat to all of Earth, and Centaurus too, from it. We've got to find out what the threat is. Someone could go there again. And anyhow—"

"Your husband was lost there," Rrinn supplied. "I heard the police lieutenant talking about it." His hands came apart, though the heavy rings remained on the wrists.

"You couldn't navigate the ship," Sibyl said. "I'll leave the laser torch with you and you can free the others. When the ship's crew finds out what Radix is like, I think—"

A tremendous blow from behind caught Sibyl off guard. She stumbled forward and found herself caught in the chains of one of the Centaurians. He managed to get his chained hands crossed around Sibyl's neck so that he was choking her.

"Have you gone mad!" Rrinn called to him, and tried to strike at him but couldn't quite reach. He began working with the torch at the body chain that held him to the floor.

Sibyl brought her knee up and kicked the Centaurian a bone-cracking blow in the knee with her foot, holding his wrists at the same time so he couldn't break her neck with one fast jerk.

The Centaurian screamed, loosened his hold and Sibyl jumped back. "He's still chlorotic," Sibyl said to Rrinn, whose hand was shaking as he held the laser torch. "Like you were. I should have remembered. There's been too much noise now. I'd better go. Don't let that one free until his chlorosis is gone."

She scuttled quickly up the stairs. Hatty would still be tied up. She smoothed her clothes and pinned her dress higher at the neck, to cover the bruises the chains had made, made her way quickly to the control room, where Joe was jotting down numbers from an astrogation handbook. He looked up in his birdlike way when she came in.

"Gee, ma'am, you look shook."

"I do?" Sibyl took a deep breath. "I forgot to arrange my face. Joe, if anybody asks, I've been in here with you for the last half hour or so, O.K.?"

"Sure," Joe pulled out a panel under the instrument board. "Have a swig, ma'am."

Sibyl took a swallow of the brandy, replaced the bottle, and had a look of polite interest on her face when Stuart slid open the door with a bang and came in with a thunderous expression on his face.

"He's been explaining to me about all those little dials. Why Stuart. I had no idea you'd *mind*."

"Joe," Stuart said, "how long has she been here? In the room with you?"

"Maybe about an hour, sir. She ain't touched nothing. Just wanted to know about the directional dials and all."

Stuart stormed out, and Sibyl said, "Well, what *are* all those dials for?"

"For navigation. Over there's the radar... uh-oh. That ain't possible." Joe went over and fiddled with the radar controls. He frowned and looked searchingly out of the observation window. Then he turned on the radio receiver.

"Now, that's funny," he said. "What was Mr. Grant upset about, ma'am, if you don't mind my asking?"

"Hatty got knocked out again. Pretty careless of Hatty, if you ask me. What's the matter with that television set?" There were spatters of sound coming through the radio receiver. "Radar," Joe corrected. "I think you'd better get Mr. Grant. We're supposed to be in deep space and there's a planetary-sized blip out there. No... there it... yes. And listen to that noise. We ought to see it through the window in a minute."

"I'll get him."

Sibyl found Stuart and Dr. Beadle in the lounge with Hatty. Hatty was red in the face and Dr. Beadle was saying, "I'll give him the truth drug if you like, but—"

"Stuart!" Sibyl cried. "How far out from Radix are we?"

"About four million miles, since we warped into space normal, why?"

"Because there's a planet out there. Furthermore it seems to appear and disappear."

"Are you feeling all right?"

"Furthermore it seems to talk on the radio. Or perhaps I got the wrong impression from what Joe said."

"*Perhaps!* Never mind about Hatty right now, Beadle. Just make sure he's all right and send him back to his post."

"All right," Dr. Beadle said when Hatty had left and the door closed, "I think you had better fill me in on what you've found out about Radix and what you were doing in the cargo hold again."

"Couldn't I have a drink first? Can you mix gin and 'gin, or only bad-tasting medicine?"

Dr. Beadle went stiffly over to the bar. "I have never," he said through his teeth, "liked women. It is unfortunate I have to deal with one. Mrs. Blue, either you are going to cooperate with me, or I shall have to tell Mr. Grant who has been attacking Hatty."

He mixed Sibyl a drink distastefully and took nothing himself.

"I didn't say I wouldn't cooperate," Sibyl said, straightening her dress across her knees, "and you're only making a fool of yourself when you threaten me. You don't know what's ahead on Radix and you may need me and you know it." Sibyl tasted her gin and 'gin, made a face because it was heavy on the 'gin, and told Dr. Beadle all that Stuart had told her. She did not tell him about the laser torch she'd given Rrinn, but only said she'd assured them they'd get help if they needed it when the ship reached Radix.

"But don't you see *we're* in no danger on Radix," Dr. Beadle said. "Or at least I'm not. Mr. Grant needs the crew—or at least a part of it—to get back. He'll certainly not want to be without a doctor."

"Thank you for being so concerned about me. I can tell it by the way you hold your mouth. But have you taken a look at the ship's stores?"

Dr. Beadle still stood up, as though it would be too great a familiarity to sit down in the same room with Sibyl. "No. There's been no occasion and I understand Mr. Grant takes personal charge of doling out the kitchen supplies. Very prudent of him."

"Yes, indeed. The rumor among the crew is that there are no stores for the trip back."

"But... perhaps he means to take on stores at Radix."

"Oh, sure. Fresh eggs, cooking sherry... Really!"

"Look!" Dr. Beadle cried suddenly. "Look at that!" He was pointing at the observation window, and Sibyl, startled, got up and went over to it.

She sucked in her breath quickly. Beyond the window, in deep space, was what looked like an enormous silver sheet flapping in the breeze. "But there *isn't* any breeze," Sibyl heard herself saying.

"Now hear this," came Stuart's voice over the intercom. "The unidentified object in view of the ship does not represent an immediate danger. It is a vegetative formation only two molecules in thickness and visible by means of cold light. Sergeant Blue, please report to the control room."

Sibyl started out of the door and then turned back to Dr. Beadle. "I think you'd better keep an eye on those Centaurians until we get to Radix. They just might do something foolish."

"They can't do anything foolish. They're chained," Dr. Beadle said. "And Hatty is guarding them."

"Watch them anyhow," Sibyl advised, hurrying out.

The control room was full of a rain of noise, and Stuart and Joe were both listening intently. Joe pressed his lips together and shook his head.

"It sounds like it might be a pattern, sir, but it sure ain't no code I know."

"Sibyl," Stuart said, "what do you make of that?"

Sibyl frowned, listening. "Nothing," she said. "What am I supposed to make of it?"

"I believe," said Stuart, "that it is a communication from Radix. The flapping screen out there is probably some sort of radar, and the noise is made by magnetic friction when the screen moves across itself. Listen to the noise again. It is not random."

Sibyl closed her eyes and listened. "Yes. It is something. But very hard to pinpoint. Like the memory a flower smell evokes. It strikes chords in the mind... Chords! That's it!" Sibyl opened her eyes. "Do you play the guitar?"

"The guitar! No."

"Piano? Ukulele?"

"I've never played anything except the stock market. For God's sake, why? Is that a symphony?"

"No. It's a G7 chord as played on the guitar by Jerry Mahoney, who went as cook on the Venture with Kenneth's expedition. Don't ask me how I know it's a G7 chord. I can only tell you that it picks up those intervals in my mind."

"G7," Stuart said, biting his lower lip. "What a message! And from the cook, you say?"

"I didn't say it was a message from Jerry. It might have been something just picked up from Jerry's mind. Or from Kenneth's mind. Kenneth played the piano. Perhaps it was considered to be an easily transmissible, universally understandable message."

"Then it was considered wrong. And it isn't a message."

"I don't know. Because Jerry always said, and Kenneth laughed and agreed with him..." Sibyl hesitated a moment, thinking of how long it had been since Jerry had said it, and how she'd been leaning on Kenneth's knee drinking a beer and watching the firelight when he said it "Jerry always said he thought the G7 chord was saying 'Good-bye Dear Friend' — GBDF — and then he'd resolve it with a C chord."

Stuart sighed. "That makes no sense at all. It should be 'Greetings!' not 'Good-bye.' If it's anything at all."

Sibyl was weeping silently inside, to think that perhaps this was all that was left of Jerry. A G7 chord, eternally unresolved. But finally, she said, "Perhaps Radix is dealing with concepts utterly alien to it, and 'hail' and 'farewell' may seem the same to it. Or perhaps Jerry or Kenneth is still alive, and sending us a warning, as Kenneth sent me the warning with the virus. Stuart," she went on, turning to him in sudden panic, "are you sure you want to go on with this?"

Stuart just looked at her.

"You're sure about everything, aren't you?" Sibyl said. "No, I haven't changed my mind. I just don't have your constant armor. Sometimes I get scared." That waving blip on the radar, that constant call on the receiver, getting louder, the sheet of light outside the observation window getting larger—

"Mr. Grant!" Joe cried suddenly, "it's following us. In fact it's catching up with us."

"Following... no. It's caught in our field because it's so light." Stuart watched the flapping sheet of light grow larger in the window. He frowned. "Joe!" he said. "How are we going to land if that thing wraps itself around the ship? Its signals are so strong we can't make an instrument landing and it's impossible to land a ship like this by the seat of your pants. We aren't even wired for it."

But Joe had been pressing buttons on his calculator, and when he looked up there was a glisten of sweat on his forehead. "You've got about fifteen minutes, boss, to do something about it, at the rate it's falling for us now."

The door to the control room was shoved open quickly, and Dr. Beadle came in carrying his black bag and closed the door and locked it behind him. He stood catching his breath for a moment, his eyes darting from Stuart's face to Sibyl's and Joe's and then back to Stuart.

He checked the lock again to make sure it was secure, and then said, almost primly, "I regret to report that there is a mutiny."

"And which side are *you* on?" Stuart asked calmly.

Dr. Beadle grimaced "Hatty was overcome by four Centaurians, who removed his keys and weapons and locked him in a cabin. The Centaurians then recruited half the crew to their side and locked up the other half. They're all scared silly about Radix and now about that white sheet out there. They are on the way to the control room now and they intend to force the navigator to turn the ship back toward

Centaurus. Despite the fact," he went on sternly with a look at Stuart, "that there seem to be no supplies for a return journey. They broke into the storeroom to look."

"And how did the Centaurians get out of the hold?" Stuart asked suspiciously.

"Someone got a laser torch to them and they burned their way out. A laser torch seems to make a good weapon, too."

There was a pounding on the door. "Open or we burn our way in!" It was Rrinn's slightly accented voice, barely audible above the rising noise of the radio. Sibyl glanced at the radar screen which was all dark now with the flapping object from Radix. The observation window was all white.

Stuart thought for thirty seconds. "Put her in space warp."

Joe shook his head. "This close to a planetary system—we might end up in the middle of its sun. You get eighty per cent target accuracy in space warp, and that's not good enough. We could better let the thing fall to the ship and then try to figure out how to get rid of it. Maybe—"

"Maybe by then the mutineers might succeed. I've been waiting weeks to land on Radix. I'm not going to get held up by miserable little problems like these. Put her in space warp."

Joe shrugged, ran his hands around the dials, and the radio noises stopped abruptly. "We'll end up either right on top of Radix or in kingdom come," he said, and the ship had barely finished shuddering into space warp when it shuddered out.

"Get flat on the floor!" Joe screamed, and Stuart went down and pulled Sibyl and Dr. Beadle with him.

"Keep out of the way of the door," Rrinn called. "I am going to use the laser torch and I don't want to kill—"

Suddenly Sibyl felt herself smashed against the floor and then she blacked out. When she came to, she heard screams in the corridor, and she stood up and felt so lightheaded she thought she might faint again.

Dr. Beadle was brushing off his trousers and Stuart was looking out of the observation window with a smile on his face.

"And what," asked Dr. Beadle, "was that?"

"That was five G's," said Joe, wiping off a mustache of perspiration. "If I hadn't done it we would have exploded in the center of Radix. I wasn't a bit sure we wouldn't anyway."

"Good work," Stuart said. "It took care of the mutiny, too."

"I think someone is dying or dead out in the corridor," Sibyl said. "Perhaps I—"

"No. We're almost there now. Look!"

Sibyl thought the ship had landed, but it was slowly circling the planet. Her eyes, accustomed to the soft illumination of the ship, at first could make out nothing but a green blur below. Then she looked again and saw a glowing green countryside going by. The ship was slowing for a touchdown and details became more and more visible.

"Countryside" wasn't the right thought. There weren't houses and trees and cows. There were odd, massive forms that might have been either green structures or structures with green growing over them. They passed a sea with odd, sheetlike things flapping out of it, reminiscent of the "radar screen" in space. But yet there was something *voiceless* about the unrolling planet.

"No animals," Sibyl said. "Perhaps they're small, or don't run in herds."

"No. No animals," Stuart agreed.

"Then where do the plants get their carbon dioxide?"

"Plant—singular. It's all one plant. It makes its own carbon dioxide. It makes everything it imagines." Stuart was staring, fascinated, at the green planet.

"That looks like a concrete landing strip," Sibyl said. They were very low now, and all they had seen so far were jungles and oceans that seemed to seethe green.

"It's something like concrete. It observed us here and spread it out for us," Stuart told her.

"It's alive?"

"Only the way your hair and fingernails are alive. It's exactly the same thing." Then Stuart was at the intercom, telling any of the crew that were still about to report to the lounge.

"But can't you tell me *now* what's going to happen?" Sibyl asked, trying to sound only curious, not desperate. "It's only a matter of minutes."

"You don't trust me?" Stuart asked sharply.

"Of course I do." He was on edge. All nerves now. She couldn't risk the faintest doubt.

The ship settled, and normal — almost normal, faintly light — gravity returned.

Sibyl stood watching by the window. The landing strip was in the midst of a luxuriant jungle. Vines like thick, plastic pipes hung from the trees, ending in wide, trumpet-like flowers. Above the jungle floated a huge, green butterfly whose wings beat with eerie tranquility. It hung headless, tailless, as though it were two joined wings and nothing else. Then it floated softly down into some unseen opening in the jungle, folding its wings as it disappeared.

Then Sibyl gasped and drew back instinctively. What looked at first like a legion of long, green snakes with weaving purple heads was crawling towards the ship from all directions.

"Don't panic," Stuart said, digging his fingers into her shoulders, unaware that in his own panic he was about to break her bones.

They hadn't been aware of the noise outside the door.

There was a circle of blue flame around the door lock, and three Centaurians and four white-faced crew members came in. Rrinn pointed the laser torch like a gun and said, "Indeed. Now we make the return journey. Blast off, navigator, or I blast you."

"No, Rrinn," Sibyl said. "Not just yet. We've got to find out something more about the nature of Radix."

"What do you mean?" Stuart asked furiously. "Not *yet*! Are you —" and he finished his sentence by slapping her across the face with the palm of his hand.

Sibyl blinked back her temper. "I was hoping the mutineers would listen to reason," she said humbly. "If not —"

Joe screamed. Rrinn had singed him lightly on the ankle.

"I don't want to torture you," Rrinn said. "But your choice is not a quick death. Lift the ship."

Joe looked at Stuart, whose eyes were on the mutineers, watching for a chance to spring at them without getting burned.

Sibyl, still sprawled on the floor where Stuart's blow had flung her, had been inching carefully toward Rrinn. Now she lunged, got his wrist in her teeth and grabbed the laser torch as he dropped it. She turned the torch on as cool as it would go and swept it lightly across the hands of the four armed crewmen. They all screamed at once and the last one got in a wild shot that went through the radar screen, making a spatter of glass.

Stuart grabbed the guns, clicked the guard off one of them and said, "O.K. Now it's my game. Into the lounge. March!"

He was back in a few moments. "Everyone is locked in the lounge. The only way out is through to port—to Radix. It's also the only way *in*."

Sibyl shuddered. "They may be back, if they see what I see out there. Will it take long—what you need to do here on Radix?"

Stuart laughed. A horrible laugh that didn't sound like him at all. "Time," he said, "is about to disappear. Don't you see? It will be an outmoded concept." He looked down at Sibyl. "Relax. I've locked the door at the end of the corridor and there isn't another laser torch."

Dr. Beadle was rubbing his hands nervously. "Still," he said, "if you want to start the communication, do it now. And then I expect to leave this planet. I don't like this, Mr. Grant. I—"

"O.K.," Stuart said. "Here go the ports." There was a deep, grinding noise. All the ports, including the whole back of the ship, were now open to Radix. "All out," Stuart said gleefully over the intercom.

"But what's going to happen to them?" Sibyl cried. "Stuart, I am responsible for sending them out of here."

"Shut up!" Stuart shouted, turning the gun on her.

Sibyl could hear screams, and a loud rustling, breaking noise. "It's *eating* them," she said, and then stuffed her fist into her mouth and bit at her knuckles, and was already frozen with horror when Stuart turned to Dr. Beadle.

"O.K., Beadle. Do what you came here to do."

"Which one?" Dr. Beadle asked.

"Joe."

Dr. Beadle got his black bag from the bunk in the corner where he'd set it.

CHAPTER VIII

"Joe," Stuart said, "come over here." He gestured with the gun.

Joe stepped forward, trying to look cocky, and pushed his hat to an insolent angle. But his grin trembled at the edges and his big dark eyes darted from Stuart to Dr. Beadle.

"What am I volunteering for?" he asked. "Sir."

Sibyl bit at her lower lip. He was so little, his bones small like a child's. Sure he was scared, with those green things snaking toward the ship, and billions of miles from anything like civilization.

"Roll up your sleeve," Dr. Beadle said.

"For what?" But he rolled it up, his eyes on Stuart's gun. Dr. Beadle brought his hand out of his black bag and while Joe was still tucking his sleeve up, Dr. Beadle jabbed a needle in his arm.

"What—" Joe started to say, but crumpled into Stuart's arms before he could finish.

"Sodium pentothal," Stuart said to Sibyl's alarmed face as he settled Joe into the navigator's seat and strapped him in. Dr. Beadle spun the seat around and started speaking to Joe in a low monotonous voice.

"You hear nothing but my voice," he said. "You will see nothing but my face."

Then Sibyl remembered. Dr. Beadle's voice through her second Radix dream. He must have come back and hypnotized her so that she spoke her dream as she dreamed. *That's* how he knew what she knew, and how Stuart believed in her dream also.

It was the voice of a professional. For the first time Sibyl felt a surge of respect for Dr. Beadle. She didn't like him any better. Indeed, he'd never seemed more loathsome. But it was obvious what he could do. The low voice went on. The room darkened greenly, the vines growing up sinuously over the window span, the trumpet flowers looking in like faces.

Sibyl was afraid she was going to scream.

Joe opened his eyes, but there was no flicker of Joe himself in them.

"I hear no voice but yours," he said.

Dr. Beadle turned and nodded at Stuart. Stuart turned and opened a small panel in the ship that Sibyl hadn't known was there. It must have been especially prepared, for Stuart withdrew a steel plug the width of the vine that now grew searchingly up and down the curved window.

In a moment a faint, very faint rustle could be heard in the pipe, and then the vine grew through. The trumpet flower uncurled itself as the vine emerged, and waved uncertainly about, as though there were a light breeze.

Stuart flipped out the clamps that anchored the navigator's chair and rolled Joe toward the bobbing flower, being careful not to get too close himself, or let it touch him.

Dr. Beadle stood in front of Joe, as close as he dared. "You are a plant of Radix," he said. "And you are speaking to Stuart Grant, commander of Earth."

Sibyl looked at Stuart. He hadn't said anything about passing himself off as commander of Earth.

The trumpet flower up close had a heavy, fleshy look, like the big purple veins in an old man. It wove about until it touched Joe's head. Then it stopped, slipped over the back of his head like an absurd woman's hat. And grew there.

"How do you get it off?" Sibyl whispered, and heard her whisper crackle through the silence of the room. Stuart flicked her a glance and licked the edge of perspiration off his upper lip.

"Sibyl!" cried Joe.

"Yes," she said. "I can't stand it any more. Stuart, you've got to get that thing off him."

Stuart looked at Dr. Beadle. "What happened?" he asked.

"Sibyl!" Joe said again.

Dr. Beadle went over to him. Joe's eyes were still glazed, unrecognizing. "Nothing. It is impossible for him to come out of it now." Dr. Beadle ran his finger over the seamless edge where the flower joined Joe's forehead.

"But why does he still recognize Sibyl?" Stuart asked.

"Because," said the voice from Joe, "I'm Kenneth. Is there no way for you to know me?"

Stuart stiffened, his hand on Sibyl's shoulder again. "Good. I hadn't dared hope it would happen so soon, that contact would be so easy to establish. Last time I lost five crew —"

"Kenneth!" Sibyl cried, wrenching her shoulder from Stuart's grasp and stepping forward. "Where are you?"

"Everywhere," he said. "I'm no longer a separate entity. And so much of me is lost. So much of my memory. I'm part of the universal mind of Radix. Here we make machines — *grow* machines — out of living matter. A biological technology. And if enough of Radix ever gets to Earth, civilization as we know it will be... digested, by Radix. For Radix, Earth is a new and valuable raw material."

"Kenneth," Stuart broke in. "Are you sure that's so bad? Have you thought that now you'll never die? You'll be forever part of the universal mind of Radix."

"I've already died," the flat voice said, from Joe's mouth, Joe's vocal cords.

"But see," Stuart went on excitedly. "Even if you're a... different shape, you're still you. You can talk to me separately from the rest of Radix."

"Only for a time. Only because it is easier for me to use Joe's mind and eyes and ears. Radix can develop its own ways of communication, in time. It is a new concept for Radix."

"Ah," said Stuart. "And *I* have something to offer Radix. I can bring Radix to Earth and Centaurus, and I can direct the formation of these worlds."

Sibyl, looking at Stuart, shivered, knowing what he was thinking.

"Kenneth," Sibyl cried, grasping the hand which was Joe's and not Kenneth's, "what can I *do*? How can I find you?"

"You can't find me. What you must do is see that Radix builds no spaceships."

"But how can I do that?"

"You can't do that," Stuart said. "The ship is here already."

"They'll use this ship? This will be Radix's spaceship?"

Stuart laughed and his eyes glistened. "*I* will be Radix's spaceship."

"Of course," Sibyl whispered. That should have been plain to her a long time ago. The whole thing. Stuart planned to become a Radix entity, make a living spaceship with himself as the brain, and go back and turn Earth into one enormous biological machine, every cell of which would be directed by Stuart alone.

What a dream of power!

This was the dream that Stuart was bringing to Radix. Radix had dreamed Radix dreams before Earthmen came. And then what human dreams it had dreamed since it took Kenneth's expedition Sibyl could guess, because she'd had them dreamed to her through the virus. But now...

"Kenneth," she said. "Radix should reject Stuart. Not take him in as part of itself. As part of Radix you —"

"As part of Radix," Joe's mouth went on, "I am ready to receive the commander of Earth and expand into new worlds. Open the rest of the ship to me. *Kill him!*"

Dr. Beadle made a strangling noise and Sibyl saw with surprise that tears were coming out of his eyes. Tears of utter fear. He was suddenly in such fear that he was unable to say whatever it was in the back of his throat.

A flicker of hope went on in Sibyl's mind. She tried to catch Dr. Beadle's eye.

"Oh, no," Stuart said, backing away a little so that he had both Dr. Beadle and Sibyl in gun range. "It's too late to change your mind." He edged back, reaching with his free hand for the switch to open all ports.

Dr. Beadle and Sibyl were standing on either side of Joe, who sat completely immobile, vegetative, speaking with the dull, flat voice of a machine.

"Open the ship to me." Then, "If you don't kill him now it will be too late. Sibyl... good-bye."

"Look!" Dr. Beadle cried suddenly. "Look at Joe!"
Joe didn't look any different, but Stuart looked.

"Look closely. Look at his eyes. You're looking at his eyes." Dr. Beadle's monotone went on and Sibyl held her breath, feeling a bursting hysteria growing within her.

"You're looking at his eyes. His eyes are looking at yours. You are his master and you keep looking at his eyes. You are looking at his eyes and hearing my voice. Joe is hearing my voice and you are hearing my voice."

The professional in Dr. Beadle had taken over completely. The exquisite skill that lives in an artist and operates independently.

I'm going to scream, Sibyl thought. In a minute I'm going to scream and ruin it all.

Stuart relaxed completely and his gun dropped from his hand and clanked on the floor and Sibyl did scream, but by that time Stuart was hypnotized.

Dr. Beadle's face was streaming with sweat. "Do you know how to close up the ship?" he asked Sibyl. "Do that and then I'll try to get Grant to blast off. Hurry."

"You must not leave Radix," Joe's flat voice said. "We want the commander of Earth. Kill him!"

Sibyl dove for the gun, but Dr. Beadle had been following her thoughts, and he got to it first. He emptied the cartridges out of it and threw them around on the floor and put the gun in his pocket. "No," he said. "We need Grant to get the ship back. Close the ports."

Sibyl went over to the instrument panel. She thought she remembered which switch it was. She wished Joe... she looked around at him and screamed, "Watch out!"

Joe had stumbled forward and had his hands around Dr. Beadle's throat just as Sibyl cried out. Dr. Beadle went down.

Sibyl opened Dr. Beadle's bag and found a scalpel and took it out of its case. Dr. Beadle was on the floor and struggling violently with Joe, whose strength was enormous now, whose fingers were digging into Beadle's neck. The vine snaked back to the tube and seemed to come out endlessly as Joe struggled.

"Kenneth!" Sibyl called, "try to be here." And she cut the tube.

"I can't," Kenneth said, through Joe.

The vine, with its mutilated end writhing, kept on growing through the tube. Joe gave a spasmodic jerk, and then pressed on at Beadle's throat, while Beadle's hands, pulling at Joe's wrists, were trembling with the exertion.

"Radix will keep you here," Joe said calmly.

"The antivirus," Dr. Beadle coughed out "The purplish capsule."

Sibyl dug in the bag. "It might not work," she said. "And I've never given a shot." But it was obvious which end the needle fitted into. She held the capsule against Joe's leg, above the sock, because that was the easiest place to get to, and thumbed the pressure plunger.

Joe screamed and a few seconds later rolled off Dr. Beadle, panting, the purple trumpet shriveling off his head. Dr. Beadle's face and neck were gorged with blood and he was gagging horribly, trying to breathe. Sibyl cut off the vine at the entrance to the tube. The cut piece flailed around and then was still. And a thought began to take shape at the back of her mind. The Radix plant was not, in its parts, immortal. But for the moment...

"Tell Stuart to plug up the tube," she said.

Dr. Beadle shook his head. He couldn't talk yet. He didn't dare give Stuart a command until he had his voice back.

Joe sat up slowly, and when he did, blood began to ooze gently from the pores in his head. "Jesus!" he said. "What was that shot you gave me, Dr. Beadle? My head..." And he took his hands away from his head and saw the blood on them, and looked around at Stuart, sitting now in a semistupor near the door, and Dr. Beadle gagging on the floor, and Sibyl, and the severed vines and the dark tangle of Radix jungle over the view window.

"Close the communication with Radix," Dr. Beadle said at last. Stuart got up uncertainly and pushed a switch and the vine cut off and lay lifeless on the deck. Stuart replaced the plug.

"Close all the locks."

Stuart pushed another switch and the ship began to vibrate at the heavy closing of the ramp at the back of the ship. And then to shake badly and— "Stop it there," Dr. Beadle commanded.

"There's too much jungle grown into the ship," Sibyl said. "We'll have to think of some way to—My God! Look!" She pointed to the control panel. A green tendril was growing out through one of the switches. It grew rapidly, a curling filament, and began to kink itself about the switches on the board.

"Blast off!" Dr. Beadle told Stuart. Stuart began slowly to reach for switches.

"But the ramps are partly open," Sibyl said. "Joe, what will happen?"

"I'm dizzy," Joe said. "I... can't you stop the blood?"

Dr. Beadle ran to his bag and pulled out a spray bottle. "Close your eyes," he said, and carefully sprayed a coagulant over Joe's face and neck. "Lie down flat on the floor. For that matter, we'd all better lie down." He took Stuart by the shoulders and sat him in the navigator's chair.

"If the ship isn't sealed," Sibyl said, "we'll die in space. Or perhaps that's what you have in mind. Perhaps that's best."

"Set the course for thirty-five thousand feet up," Dr. Beadle told Stuart. "I have no intention of dying. I want to throw off the jungle."

Joe was flat on the floor. "If you blast off with the ramp open," Joe said, "the ship will be unbalanced and the gyros won't work. It'll nose over, maybe, or get off the ground then crash. If you want to try it, you better let me do it."

Dr. Beadle got Stuart out of the chair and onto the deck, and Joe took over. He pulled down a big lever slowly and sucked loudly at his teeth. There was a deep, tearing noise that came through the hoarse straining of the engines.

Stuart began trying to sit up straight, bracing himself with his hands against the trembling of the ship. Sibyl watched him carefully, and slipped off one of her sharp-heeled shoes. If the ship crashed back to Radix, she'd have to kill him fast, and keep him from the Radix plant until his brain died.

"Why do we need Stuart to get us back to Earth," she asked Beadle, "if we have Joe?"

"Because I'm not sure Joe—" He stopped because the ship was suddenly off the ground with a violent lurch, climbed to thirty-five thousand feet by the altimeter, and stayed there.

The vines still clung to the windows, so thickly that only a few beams of the dazzling sunshine of Radix got through. Then they began to slip slowly off.

"The ramps are closed," Joe said with a grin. "We're all right."

"No, we're not," Sibyl said, worriedly. "I think we should have—" But she was turning and she found Stuart on his feet, a curious smile on his face. Dr. Beadle was getting up, too, and he looked up into Stuart's fist. Sibyl could have screamed a warning, but she didn't.

Instead, she leaped at Stuart's back as Dr. Beadle hit the deck with a crash. She caught Stuart off balance, sent him over on all fours, and clung to his shoulders with one thumb on his jugular vein. He went down, rolled over on top of Sibyl, but she moved her body out of the way just in time, keeping her thumb dug into his neck, pressing his big vein flat. He reached back for her head with one hand, tore at her oppressive thumb with the other and fainted before he could get her off.

"Joe!" Sibyl shouted. "Land the ship! Quickly! Anywhere!"

She dug frantically into Beadle's bag, found the packet of capsules, one gone, marked *Sodium Pentothal*. She slipped the capsule into a needle and plunged it into Stuart's arm.

Joe was at the instrument panel and Sibyl could feel the ship coming down quickly.

"What do you think you're doing?" Dr. Beadle cried. "We just got away from Radix by the sheerest luck."

"The lady says bring it down, I bring it down," Joe answered, turning a knob that made the motor louder and slower. The ship's landing wings were out and Sibyl could see the edge of one as the ship veered for landing.

"Go *up*," Dr. Beadle shouted, pointing his gun at Joe and backing up to include Sibyl.

"You took all the bullets out so nobody could shoot Stuart, remember?" Sibyl said. "That was sodium pentothal I gave him. I could have killed him and maybe I should have, but I've been cooking up an idea. A crazy idea, maybe, but I need your help."

"You fool! There's only one thing to do and that's get away from this monstrous planet as fast as we can."

"No. Now we know something about the nature of Radix." Sibyl pulled at the vine tendril that now hung limp over the control board. "See. It's just a plant. Unless it's free-flying in form it can't live without roots somewhere. And if it *is* free-flying I venture to say it can't live without light and water. I know a way we can keep Stuart and still have him under control, without having to rely on a hypnotic trance, which you just saw him break out of."

The ship settled into a mass of vegetation so heavy it cradled the enormous steel hulk. Immediately inquisitive vines began to grow up over the view port.

"I don't like it," Beadle said. Rivulets of perspiration ran down his forehead, as he watched the purple blossom, the heavy, curious flower searching the window. "What do you want me to do?"

"Help me get Stuart into the chair," Sibyl said. "Not you, Joe. Go sit on the bunk and save your strength. Dr. Beadle, be ready to hypnotize him as he comes out. I want his mind completely under your control when the Radix viruses enter it."

And already Stuart's eyes were beginning to flicker. "You hear nothing but my voice," Dr. Beadle began. He was holding Stuart upright in the chair.

Sibyl pushed back the opening to the tube which led outside and removed the plug. She watched through the view port while one of the fleshy, purple flowers moved blindly in the right direction. Then there was a rustle in the tube and the flower grew through, opening as it emerged, and then it swayed down slowly until it settled on Stuart's head.

There was a retching noise from Joe. Sibyl looked up and then away. He was being very sick, and he wept with spasms.

Dr. Beadle, still talking softly and slowly, glanced at Joe, who now had a trickle of blood running where he'd scratched off a bit of the skin spray. Then Beadle glanced at Sibyl, reminding her that she was responsible for this. For bringing them back. For Joe being sick. For this horror that was being done to Stuart.

Sibyl swallowed hard and pushed away a desperate wish to be just a woman. To let Dr. Beadle or Joe decide things. To curl up and be comforted. To wrest the flower from Stuart's head before it was too late, and follow him anywhere, even into death; or what was worse, the endless anonymity of being part of Radix, where there was no release of death.

"Tell him he's Radix now. Radix under your control."

Dr. Beadle spoke on softly, commanding Radix. Stuart sat slumped in the chair, the flower growing down seamlessly into his forehead.

"Be sure it's Radix," Sibyl whispered. "Be sure you've got communication with it. Ask it... ask it... just tell it to talk."

"Were you injured?" Dr. Beadle asked Stuart-Radix. "Do you feel pain?"

"We have not manufactured that concept yet. However we sort out what you mean."

"Ask it how it sends messages, how it communicates," Sibyl said.

"How do you communicate?" Dr. Beadle asked. "How do you send a message in a human brain?"

"Before we had digested and taken apart a human brain we could not have communicated. But in digesting a mind, we learned it, and from the first men who landed we extracted molecules enabling us to manufacture viruses viable in human chemistry. We have no eyes, no ears, no voice. But all these things we learned of and more, so much more, from human men. All parts of human men we can use, and manufacture things from them."

"What does 'manufacture' mean?"

"Directing our growth, of course. That is the purpose of all life. To grow better and more interesting forms. And so encountering animal chemistry for the first time opened a whole new world for us. So, having thought the thoughts of men and knowing something about them, we were prepared for the second expedition, which we were sure would come sooner or later. We had a virus ready, and instead of digesting the men, we communicated with one. As now, growing into his brain so as to have a free flow of viruses back and forth. We do not hear your voice. We only get the meaning which registers in this man's brain as you speak. But we are working on seeing and hearing devices, and many other things. And so we need human parts. So also we are glad you brought back the commander of Earth."

Sibyl looked around at Joe. He had fallen asleep in exhaustion, his head on his arms at the instrument panel. Blood trickled from his head again, snaking down his neck.

A slow seepage. Dr. Beadle ought to see to it immediately. But Dr. Beadle couldn't be spared. Not yet.

"Give it a command to go to sleep," Sibyl said. And held her breath. Because if all of Radix could be commanded like this...

"You will go to sleep," Dr. Beadle said. "You are tired and you go to sleep ..."

"It is not night," Radix answered, Stuart's limp mouth moving mechanically, horribly, like a corpse wired to be a ventriloquist's dummy.

"Night is falling," Dr. Beadle went on. "Night is falling. Darkness is coming. It is getting cooler. The sun is going away." On he talked, until Sibyl felt herself falling to sleep.

"It is not night," Radix said suddenly. "Surely you do not expect to deceive us. We feel the sunlight."

Sibyl sat up with a jerk. "No go," she said. "What I had thought was... Oh, never mind. We can still go ahead with my plan. But Kenneth..." She went up to Stuart, clasping his cool, sleeping hands, rubbing his wrists softly as though he were Kenneth and needed to be waked gently. "Kenneth, even if I can't find you, isn't there something you can say to me after ten years?"

Stuart's lips moved, started to speak, stopped, then started again. "Only that I love you and that I am lost. So lost. Everything is gone but memory of memory and even that grows cool and dim. Even my memory of myself grows dim and cool, and I call to myself and I call to you. But I have no voice, no eyes, no ears. Seeing you through the eyes of Stuart Grant, the image of you I find in his mind, is not my memory of your memory."

"Then good-bye," Sibyl said. "Dr. Beadle, I'll be right back. Keep everything as it is." She headed for the hydroponic garden, where round eggplant gleamed lushly in the fluorescent light and tomatoes leaned heavy and red from their vines. She disconnected one of the plastic pots of vermiculite from the pipe that fed in its nutrients, and hurried back to the control room with it. The pot was heavy and seeped dampness onto her from where the pipe had been.

"Now," Sibyl said to Dr. Beadle, "you see what I have in mind."

Dr. Beadle stared at her and frowned. "You're mad," he said. "If we'd just kept going everything would have been all right." Then Beadle's face changed. "You fool! You did this only in the hope of finding your husband. You endangered all our lives, and even all of Earth, for this sentimental gesture."

"Tell Stuart to get up and walk over here. Tell him he's Stuart again. I need more length on the vine."

There was an odd, piercing noise as Stuart got up. A noise like crackling bells, and Sibyl looked up to see Joe convulsed with laughter, giggling horribly and holding on to the back of his chair. He was bleeding more now.

Dr. Beadle went to his bag. "Stop it, Joe. You're loosening your spray bandage. You ought to be in bed but you've got to navigate the ship."

"I didn't do it *only* on account of Kenneth," Sibyl said. "It's a way to control Stuart."

Beadle held Joe's head still with one hand and applied the spray with the other. "Keep your eyes closed. Relax as much as possible. I'll give you a tranquilizer after you get us off this planet and on course. Meanwhile you have to control yourself."

Sibyl got out Beadle's scalpel, shut her eyes briefly against the cruel, razor gleam of its edge, and cut the vine where it emerged from the tube. Then she slammed shut the opening, plugged it, and ran to the vermiculite with the cut end of the vine.

A whitish ooze bled out on her hand. She plunged one fist into the vermiculite, making a hole, and then gently planted the cut vine, pushing the fluffy, damp vermiculite around the plant.

Stuart swayed. Sibyl braced herself against him and let him down gently onto the floor. She dragged the blanket off the bunk and put it around him because he felt so cold. But he shouldn't be dying! Joe hadn't died. Hadn't even changed when the vine was first cut.

The room was darkening quickly, where the vegetation pushed blindly, insistently at the port. Green shadows flicked through the room as a breeze blew outside, and Joe said, "I'm scared. Tell you the truth, I'm scared."

"O.K., Joe, I think you can take off now."

"Wait!" Dr. Beadle said. "I don't know what's going on in his metabolism, but if he's to have any chance of survival I'll have to give him something so he doesn't produce antibodies against the Radix infestation."

"Nobody has, have they?"

"Nobody's undergone a wholesale invasion such as you're planning for him. Even Joe — we gave him the antivirus in time — or perhaps not in time." Dr. Beadle glanced at Joe, who was calm now, and adjusting switches on the control board.

Dr. Beadle got out a needle and two capsules. "The other is to slow down his metabolism," he explained. "His processes will be at half energy, whether he's awake or asleep."

Dr. Beadle gave the shots, got another ready, and lay down next to Stuart, one hand on Stuart's pulse. "Take off slow," he told Joe. "As slowly as possible. You can accelerate later. If Stuart's heart stops beating I'll try the adrenalin. Sibyl, you took too much on yourself, starting all this without consulting me first. I had no way to make medical preparations."

"If I'd consulted you first you'd have refused." There was a roaring from the engines and the huge ship tore out from the vines and thrust into the sky and Sibyl felt the flattening of her lungs and steadied Stuart's limp body, watching that the vine end did not slip out of its pot. The thrust of the ship went on, built up, and then cut off as the ship began its endless fall through space.

"Can you cut the ship's gravity to a half G?" Dr. Beadle asked.

Joe nodded, adjusted dials; and Sibyl, getting up, felt the sudden lightness and almost smiled in spite of everything. She felt the weight a child feels, and remembered suddenly what it was like to jump over a fence, and not to have to wear a brassiere.

Dr. Beadle got to his feet, dusted off his trousers meticulously. "A half G will keep a lot of strain off his heart. And mine too, for that matter. I think his pulse is all right."

"We need to get him immediately to the hydroponic garden," Sibyl said. "If you get the stretcher out of the dispensary the two of us can carry him and the vermiculite at a half G."

"Yes. But first I've got to see to Joe. He can't go on much longer and if we lost Joe before we bring Stuart around... you can see where that leaves us." Dr. Beadle pursed his thin lips.

"I can see how concerned you are over Joe's welfare," Sibyl said. "I don't suppose you care that Joe has a wife at home waiting for him. And that he's going to be a father."

Dr. Beadle had his hand on Joe's pulse. "I don't care or not care. The effect is the same." He let go of Joe's wrist and began winding the blood pressure strap around Joe's arm. "Joe, is there a warning signal if the ship's running into danger?"

Joe nodded. "A siren and that red light. Usually means a meteor swarm or a magnetic storm."

"Then we can listen and watch for it. And I won't put you so far asleep that you can't be waked up."

Joe set the course for Sol and then bedded down in a bunk in the control room. Dr. Beadle cleaned his head off again, resprayed, gave him a series of shots. Then shook his head. "He ought to have blood. But you and I are both the wrong types."

"What about Stuart?"

"Stuart's whole system is in shock. I can't chance it, for either him or Joe. I don't know what's happening to Stuart's blood chemistry and I haven't the equipment to find out."

In the hydroponics room Stuart lay unconscious across the bed of vermiculite, a blanket across him; the vine from his head led into a pot of vermiculite and it looked wilted. Sibyl found the room controls, turned up the humidity and turned down the light intensity.

Dr. Beadle set up a bottle of glucose on a stand and tucked the needle into a vein in Stuart's arm. Then he set a metal table against Stuart's chest, taped it on, and led the wires from it to a small black box.

"I'm going to do this for Joe, too," he told Sibyl. "Come look. It indicates danger if the pulse, respiration or temperature go above or below those red lines. Then you call me immediately. We're going to have to sleep in shifts. We'll wake up Joe every twelve hours to check out the ship, and if there's an emergency. And when you wake Joe up, please have him a high protein meal ready."

Sibyl nodded, increased the heat to seventy-five degrees in the plant room. "If the tomatoes ripen too fast I'll can them. You can sleep first. I want to keep an eye on the Radix plant. These first hours may make the difference between life and death. And I want to check the ship's stores. Joe said they were low, but he was thinking in terms of a crew of forty. There are only three — four — of us left. If necessary we can live off vegetables from the hydroponic garden." Sibyl searched among the garden supplies and found a rooting hormone. She applied it half-strength and covered the vine with a piece of plastic to reduce wilting from transpiration. No use starting the feedings until there were roots.

Sibyl's days were eight hours long, her nights eight hours long, and she stayed too busy to think much. She bathed both Stuart and Joe every day and did all the cooking because Dr. Beadle made it plain that he did not do these menial chores. She took care of the hydroponic garden, varying the light intensities for the tomatoes and pumpkins and beans, following the instructions in a book which hung on a chain by the door.

There was no book for Radix, however, and Sibyl watched the rooting vine as though it were a sick baby. For a week it looked as though it might curl up and die, and the bracts behind the purple flower that enveloped Stuart's head wilted and fell off. Sibyl cautiously added another solution of rootone and some vitamin B1 to the vermiculite.

Stuart's pulse, respiration and temperature fell constantly.

Dr. Beadle tended to Stuart's intravenous feeding. He and Sibyl saw each other only briefly, when one was waking the other up. It was Beadle who waked Joe, gave him the meal Sibyl left prepared, supported him and, as he got weaker, carried him over to the instrument panel to check their course.

Sibyl tried to read the navigation manuals, tried to figure out what all the dials and switches on the instrument panel were for. But it was hopeless. They had to depend on Joe or Stuart. And Joe was dying and Stuart wasn't coming back to life yet.

Impatiently, one evening—evening, ship time, with a half hour to go before she could wake up Dr. Beadle—Sibyl slammed shut a book named *Orbit Calculations* and went back to have one more look at Stuart's vine. It was looking healthier and Sibyl thought she could see it beginning to vein green under the skin of Stuart's jaw, but she wasn't sure. Very carefully, knowing it would be better to wait than disturb the plant, but not able to wait, Sibyl turned back the vermiculite a bit at a time, and took a quick breath. Roots! It had rooted. Healthy, thrusting roots clustered around the sharp cut. Now it should grow quickly.

And it was important that it should not grow *too* quickly.

Excited, Sibyl got out a large plastic cup, mixed an antauxin and as heavy a dose of plant food as she dared use. She'd never fed it before because she was afraid of burning it in case the roots hadn't started.

She poured in the antauxin and plant food, then turned up the light intensity. Not too high. But the plant should be able to take a good bit more light now.

It should grow quickly now, as it did on Radix, but limited by the antauxin. Perhaps before her eyes. Sibyl decided to take two more hours on her waking time. Dr. Beadle shouldn't object to that. She bent over the Radix plant, used now to the strange slumber of Stuart's face, his limp body cradled in the almost coffinlike plant box. She glanced back at the box registering Stuart's respiration and temperature. It had been below the red line for three days now, but Dr. Beadle said it was still safe, as long as there was no *sudden* change.

The plant food should be reaching the roots now, rising osmotically through the tiny, multiplying cells. And the light now should be stimulating—

There was a wild shrieking from the control room through the intercom. Sibyl's hand sprang to her throat in fear, in surprise.

CHAPTER IX

Sibyl ran to the control room. In the dimness the warning light flashed. On, off, on, off, and the color and sound were the color and sound of fear.

"Joe!" she cried, and shook him. "Joe! Wake up!"

Joe opened his eyes and looked up at her weakly, his mouth slack, his eyes half-conscious, closing them against the blatant winking of the light. His face was pasty and his hair hung lank and uncut around his bony face.

Sibyl ran to the door, switched on the overhead light, ran to Dr. Beadle's room and met him coming down the hall. Always meticulous, he'd stopped to dress before he came out, and Sibyl was so irritated by the perfect crease in his trousers she almost forgot for a moment what she was doing.

"Emergency," she said, and let him get by her and go first down the hall. He carried his black bag and if he were in a hurry it didn't show. Sibyl was glad she'd seen him scared, really scared, that once on Radix. Otherwise she'd have had no way of knowing he was human.

Dr. Beadle leaned over Joe, who'd gone back to his dark sleep, and gave him a shot. "I don't usually give him adrenalin like this, but we can't wait for him to wake up slowly."

Joe sat up, began breathing quickly, shook himself like a dog coming out of water. He leaped up and went over to the control board and pushed a switch, cutting off the awful sound and flashing light. Then, smoothly, he cut on the motors and Sibyl could feel the extra gravity as the ship began to change course.

Joe's hands moved quickly, expertly, over the instrument panel,

115

as though it were a familiar musical instrument.

"Magnetic storm ahead," he said.

"What would happen," Sibyl asked, "if we got caught in it?"

"Tear the ship to pieces at worst. At best, make jackstraws out of the directional dials so we'd never know which way was out. Ain't no need to be scared now. We veer around it. I keep the ship on manual until we get around it."

"Then we're off course now?"

"Ain't no other way to veer. But don't worry, I'll—"

Joe stood up suddenly, clutched at his chest and said, "It's come! This is it!"

And fell down dead.

Dr. Beadle ran to him, needle in hand, and then stood back, shaking his head. "No chance. I've kept him alive on drugs for a month. There's nothing left to drug now."

Tears came to Sibyl's eyes. She went over to Joe and cradled his head softly. "Poor Joe," she said. They had known he would die but somehow Sibyl hadn't quite believed it. She pulled his wallet out of his pocket. A dim picture of a rather plump young woman. Identification cards. Membership card in American Bowlers.

All there was of Joe.

Sibyl saved it. She'd see to the wife if she ever got home. She began thinking of what to tell her, trying to remember everything Joe had ever said about her.

"Later!" Dr. Beadle snapped at Sibyl. "Do you realize we're off course! We headed away from Sol and now we could fall through space forever, at God knows what speed."

Sibyl laid Joe down gently, stood and looked helplessly at the instrument panel and then at Dr. Beadle.

"We've got to revive Stuart," he said.

"But it's too soon! The roots are just forming and you know how his metabolism has been."

"If we wait any longer we're all doomed. We have no way of knowing where we're headed, and if our fuel will hold out even if we get back on course."

"O.K. We can try." Sibyl followed Dr. Beadle down the lonely halls of the ship and into the warm, humid hydroponic garden, and she heard him gasp as he went up to Stuart.

If Stuart were dead, then they were all dead. Sibyl closed her eyes in a brief prayer and went over to the lighted trough where Stuart lay. And drew a quick breath, her hand flying to her throat involuntarily.

For the vine had, indeed, responded to the plant food, and had grown green veins under Stuart's skin, down his neck, along his hands where they lay at his sides, and white roots reached from his wrists into the white vermiculite.

Dr. Beadle knelt and pulled the blanket down from Stuart's chest. Stuart's skin was so pale now, the black hair on his chest looked startling. And he'd lost weight, so that his ribs knobbed under the white skin. And below the skin grew a pale spread of green vine, very pale, for the cover had kept the light out. Roots were growing out along his back.

"I used an antauxin," Sibyl said. "And still see how fast it grew! I could use more. And decrease the light and temperature."

Dr. Beadle had his stethoscope out, did a quick examination, pulled up Stuart's eyelid, sighed. "I don't know what drugs to use. I'm afraid—"

Then Sibyl gave a little scream. Stuart's eyes were suddenly open, staring cold and hard at Dr. Beadle and Sibyl. "Where am I? Where is the rest of my world?"

"You're on our ship, headed for Earth. If we can get there. Right now we're off course," Dr. Beadle said. "We want to talk to Stuart, not you, Radix. We need information."

"We want to return to our world," Radix said, "and make certain preparations before we invade Earth. And we do not want the dwarfing hormone in our food. We cannot grow properly."

"That's impossible. Unless you release Stuart's mind so that we can talk to him, we will fall through space forever. We will all die."

"Instead we will go back to Radix. We will release information from Stuart Grant to take us back to Radix. What are the readings with reference to Alpha Centauri?"

Dr. Beadle turned on Sibyl. "You *see!*" he said. "You see how well your plan worked! Now there is nothing to save us."

Sibyl reached over and switched off the light, plunging the room suddenly into total darkness.

"What—"

"Wait," Sibyl said. "The plant will go to sleep, and then we can reach Stuart's mind. If you had been able to keep the Radix mind under control with hypnotism it would have been so much simpler. But we can manage this way."

"I'll catch Stuart when he comes out of half-sleep. If he does."

But there was no sound from Stuart, except the almost imperceptible sound of his breathing. "Stuart Grant, do you hear me?" And Dr. Beadle talked on, but Stuart did not make a sound, change the rhythm of his breathing at all.

"Damn!" said Beadle. "I'll have to try a stimulant. I don't like it." He rummaged in his black bag. "Take the flashlight and hold your hand over the light. I only need to see for a moment. Turn it off after I give the shot. We don't want to bring the Radix mind out of quiescence."

Getting navigational instructions from Stuart, and carrying them out, was infinitely more difficult than Sibyl could have imagined. She didn't know the names of the dials or what they were for. She drew a picture of the dials, brought it down, put on the light briefly so Stuart could stare at them with his dead eyes, went back up, read numbers over the intercom, pushed switches and buttons and then wasn't sure it was right.

It seemed to go on for hours. Stuart's odd, flat, hypnotized voice giving the instructions, Sibyl growing terribly weary, because all this had started at the end of her eight-hour stretch and hour after hour had gone by uncounted. Stuart grew weary, the stimulant wore off and twice Dr. Beadle had to renew his shots and then told Sibyl that Stuart couldn't stand any more. As though Sibyl were purposefully slowing things up.

But finally things checked out as they ought to. Only Sibyl still wasn't finished. She stopped at the galley to get herself a cup of coffee and one for Dr. Beadle, hurried on down to the hydroponic garden, switched on the light.

Dr. Beadle had his hand on Stuart's pulse, shook his head. "I don't know," he said. "I just don't know. I've taken a sample of his blood to analyze. Maybe I can make some sense out of it. The vine is growing along his nerve trunks, not his veins."

Sibyl handed Beadle his coffee. He looked at the rim of the cup as though suspecting it had not been properly washed, wiped it delicately with a clean handkerchief. "I will have breakfast and then see to Joe's space burial. Get to sleep as soon as you can. I cannot cope by myself if you become ill."

"Why, do I look bad?"

"Yes. Finish up what you have to do and I will wake you in eight hours."

Alone in the bright humid room Sibyl bent over the Stuart-Radix complex and thought, with no emotion at all, of how she had been in love with Stuart. Of how those still, slack lips had kissed and how that chest and those shoulders had felt under her hands. But now he was nothing, only a flat memory as dull as a bad painting. As fake as bad music that tries to be sad about something that isn't sad.

Sibyl mixed up another solution of antauxin, poured it all around the Stuart-Radix roots. She decreased the light intensity, set the temperature at fifty-five degrees. It wouldn't be good for the tomatoes, but there was enough food left in the freezer for the rest of the two weeks until they got home.

Home.

Sibyl waked up with long, dark shapes of dreams still moving in her mind. Dr. Beadle stood over her, a damp cloth in his hand.

"It's about time," he said. His clothes were rumpled, his eyes were red, and he had a scrubby growth of reddish beard that went oddly with his babyish eyebrows.

Sibyl blinked, sat up, and felt suddenly terribly weak.

She frowned. "How different you look!" she said. "What on earth happened?"

"You've been out for a week," Dr. Beadle said. "You picked up some disease fooling with that Radix plant. I had to tie you down for a while. I've had only a wink of sleep now and then. And we've been off course for twelve hours and Stuart won't answer me. Radix has infested his brain completely. Probably after we used him with hypnotism."

Sibyl swung her legs off the side of the bunk, waited a moment while the dizziness cleared. "You didn't get the virus, too?"

"I haven't been handling the Radix plant. When I touch Stuart I wear rubber gloves. And I never let patients breathe on my mouth," he finished up rather primly.

"So Stuart doesn't talk. Is he still alive?"

Dr. Beadle shrugged "Not in the ordinary way. But yes, he breathes and his heart beats. His temperature is fifty-five degrees. Nobody else with a temperature like that is alive. Here, drink this."

Sibyl drank that—a warm mixture that tasted like broth and smelled like a drugstore.

"There's some more in the refrigerator; if you feel weak, drink as much as you like. I've got to get some sleep. If you feel absolutely too weak to stay awake, wake me up. But remember I've been going on sheer nerve for a week and I *must* rest. If you can think of some way to get the ship back on course, do it." And Dr. Beadle stumbled off to his cabin, sighing deeply.

Sibyl sat on the edge of the bed until the broth went down and she felt stronger. Then she got up and inspected the control board. The navigation chart was there, for all the good it did. She could tell the dials were not pointing the right way, but how to get them to change back?

She went to the hydroponics room, stopping on the way for another cup of broth in the galley. The extreme weakness, the lassitude, were leaving her now, and she felt the surge of unaccountable joy that sometimes rose in her when things were at their worst, that made all things, even death, seem unimportant in the face of the momentary sheer pleasure of existence.

Dr. Beadle had failed to prepare Sibyl for what she saw in the hydroponics room.

For Stuart had grown. He was bloated to twice his ordinary size and extended greenly over the sides of the trough in which he lay. His eyes, wide open, stared coldly at the ceiling and the lids were grown back against his eyebrows. From the root of the vine, which extended beyond Stuart's head into the flower pot where Sibyl had thrust it when she cut it from the Radix planet, grew a blunt-leaved, stunted plant.

Sibyl switched off the light, thinking as she did of how that light must feel to Stuart's peeled eyes, and she waited a few minutes.

"Stuart!" she called then. "Stuart Grant." She swallowed, steeled herself. "Darling." But there was no answer. Only the faint rustle that Stuart's breathing motions made in the vermiculite on which he lay.

Sibyl turned the light back on, increased the intensity and the heat. There was only one more thing to try. "Kenneth," she called, "Kenneth, are you there in any way?"

"Yes," Stuart's voice answered stiffly. "We want to return to our world. We want more light. More food. You, too, may become Radix. Power, immortality wait for you."

"Stuart wants those things, not me. If you will navigate us the rest of the way to Earth, you will be received by our government as a foreign power and trade treaties can be arranged. And then you can return to your world as part of the Federation of the Worlds, Radix and Centaurus and Earth."

But what _would_ happen if Radix survived all the way to Earth, Sibyl wondered. Would this horrible plant be considered a foreign power or a dangerous parasite?

"Sibyl," Stuart's voice went on, "I'm part of Radix now. Part of the Universal Mind. Stuart Grant _is_ Radix. And I will navigate the ship back to Radix. You have no choice. Return to Radix or die falling through space forever. Death isn't better, Sibyl. Radix can absorb you and it's like swimming. Like swimming far out until finally you become liquid and part of the sea. And float forever."

So Stuart's mind was gone. Well, it was bound to. Sibyl wondered why she'd thought it could be kept separate. She'd relied on the hypnotism. But Radix had understood it too soon.

Sibyl thought about returning to Radix, giving up. Would it be so bad?

Of course it would. Sibyl rubbed her forehead with the back of her hand. It would mean returning Stuart, with all his dreams of power, to the planet Radix. It meant Radix would build its living spaceship and invade Earth and soon all of Earth and Centaurus too would be Stuart-Radix. And eventually perhaps all of the universe.

"No," said Sibyl. "There are things worse than death." And looked with loathing at the green and purple horror that had been her lover, Stuart Grant.

Death for all of them. Sibyl could turn off the light, cut off the water, and let the Radix plant die. It would be the safe way, because if it lived on after she and Dr. Beadle it might outgrow its bounds with Sibyl not there to supply the antauxin, and then, if there were fuel left, either go back to Radix, or on to Earth with no one to prepare for it, and there explode into millions of viruses or spores or... There were too many ways.

She'd talk to Dr Beadle about it. But then there was the chance that he'd rather return to Radix than die. He was a man of no loyalties. Still—it would be easy enough to kill the plant while Beadle was asleep. Unless he could foresee she would do this and dispose of her first. Perhaps, Sibyl finally decided, the safest thing would be to poison this Radix plant right then. With what? An overdose of plant food? Oh, anything. The bottle of disinfectant in the kitchen. Pure chlorine. That would do it.

Sibyl closed the door behind her, went to the kitchen, got the chlorine. Here went the last, faint, wild hope of ever getting home. Always, now, death would be with her and Dr. Beadle. And what was it going to be like, those last days?

Then: "Sibyl!" over the intercom. Or was that the word?

It was a rustling noise that somehow managed to sound like... like Kenneth calling her in her green dreams. "Sh... sh... Sibyl." Softly.

Sibyl put the chlorine bottle down and rushed back to the plant room.

Leaves fluttered. But what moved? Carefully keeping her distance from Stuart, from that infectious mass of vegetation, she searched.

"Sh... sh... Sibyl!"

It was the blunt-leaved plant in the pot. It moved, rustled in no breeze. She bent closer to it. Kenneth's intonation. Not his voice, really, but something Kenneth-like about it.

Sibyl reached for the pruning knife, cut the umbilicus from Stuart's head to the plant that grew in the pot. The cut vine length twisted back, as though in agony, and plunged into the vermiculite at Stuart's side.

"Sh... Sibyl. That was right." The faintest whisper from the blunt-leaved plant. "I've got control here for the moment. Quick, up to the control room and I'll tell you how to move the switches. Call to me the numbers on each dial from right to left."

"But can't I just bring you up there? If it's too heavy I can wake Dr. Beadle to help me."

"No, too cold. Not light enough. This takes tremendous effort. Other forces to be overcome and viruses are mutating right now. I won't last. Hurry! And then destroy all this. Every cell. Now go."

"Yes." Sibyl knelt by the shuddering plant, wanting to touch it. Yes, she would. "But Kenneth, where *are* you? What are you talking with? Listening with? Oh, my darling."

And gently pushed aside the leaves, to find a purple growth, almost a flower, with almost the face and features of Kenneth. Kenneth growing a vegetative self.

"Yes," she said, and wept as she ran to the control room.

"Ready," she said, turning the intercom up to maximum so she could hear his whispers. She read off the dials and the fluttery voice came back at her. "Push the switch by the azimuth dial until it registers two hundred one. Watch the fuel flow dial to your lower left. If it goes below eighteen, push the azimuth switch the other way until the fuel flow comes above eighteen. O.K.?"

"O.K.," Sibyl said. "It stays above eighteen."

"The altitude dial next. Be ready to adjust the azimuth dial if the needle goes off two hundred one. The altitude…"

On the voice went. Then it faded out, came back, faded out again. But finally the ship was on course again and Sibyl got up and realized as she did how terribly weak she was again. She'd been in bed for seven days and then all this strain on top of it.

She'd have another bowl of that broth and then get back to Kenneth. With Kenneth's mind left, surely there was some way to get to him to save him.

Sibyl grabbed for support as she went down, fainting from weakness, knowing she was blacking out and fighting it, trying to call out to wake Dr. Beadle, but the blackness came.

And sometime later she half waked, and then dreamed herself going into the garden — it turned into a garden she had once had long ago — and finding Kenneth and telling him, Oh, Kenneth, I had such a dream of such a flower!

And slept smiling, through long, dim hours as the ship hurtled through the immensities of space, and in the hydroponics room, under the damp blanket of bright heat, mutated viruses swarmed into the valiant remains of what had been Kenneth's mind.

"Sibyl! Mrs. Blue!" It was Dr. Beadle standing over her, toeing her to see if she were conscious. "I waked up and twelve hours had gone by. Did you faint?"

Sibyl sat up painfully. "My arm hurts. I must have been lying on it. Yes. I fainted and then I must have slept. Oh, I'm so *hungry*."

"Don't get up yet. I'll bring you something. Then move slowly and don't overdo it. You must have done something foolish."

"I got the ship back on course."

Dr. Beadle's eyebrows went up. "Are you raving?"

"No. When you bring my broth I'll tell you about it."

He was off, padding down the hall in bedroom slippers, still in pajamas, with such a growth of whiskers he was well on the way to a beard.

Sibyl finished the broth and her story together. "So I think," she said, "I think we really might make it back to Earth. We're just nine days away — three were added by getting off course — and if we don't run into anything else we'll be within radio distance of Earth in five days. Then they can send a ship after us or get somebody to radio landing instructions. But right now I want to go into the hydroponics room and kill the Radix plant. And see if I can save the part where Kenneth's mind is."

"Don't get too close to any part of it," Dr. Beadle said, and went back to his cabin to dress and shave.

"You'd shave and dress," Sibyl said after him, "if you knew you had ten minutes before you disintegrated."

But Sibyl went briefly back to her cabin to comb her hair and fix her face and rouge her knees. As though Kenneth really might be waiting in the garden, to see her after ten years.

She tried to push open the door to the hydroponics room, but something was holding it closed. Something yielding, so that the door gave a little, but didn't open. A little trickle of cold thought began in Sibyl's mind.

There was a strong smell that came through the door. The fishy, vitaminy smell of plant food. But she had hardly used any at all.

Only enough to keep... She stood back from the door, her hand to her throat. The bright lights had been on all that time, both the blue for growth and the far red for blossoming. Twelve hours. And no one to check or add antauxin or to clip away tendrils and buds... Oh, but surely it wouldn't have grown so fast.

The door began to open inward, slowly, and a green snake reached out.

"Dr. Beadle!" Sibyl screamed, turned, and ran pell- mell down the hall, the green snaking after her and a mass of vegetation bushing out behind it. The light overhead brightened, and Sibyl looked back briefly, to see the doorway now hidden in green and searching tendrils up and down the walls, where switches were.

The Radix voices — Stuart's dead voice — came over the intercom. "Don't be afraid, Sibyl. Come back. Come back to Kenneth."

Would Kenneth say that? Had something developed she didn't know anything about, like Kenneth taking over the Radix mind... but no. That was the Stuart voice. Sibyl ran on, through the kitchen, up the stairs to Dr. Beadle's cabin, yanked the door open and closed it behind her, leaning her back against it and trembling.

"It's so horrible," she moaned. "The voice, and all that growing, reaching thing..."

Dr. Beadle adjusted his necktie by the mirror and turned to her with a frown of his little eyebrows. "What's so horrible? What is it? I told you to take it easy."

Sibyl swallowed hard, got herself under control. "The Radix plant," she said. "I'd left the light intensity turned up and somehow it suddenly... grew. The way it does on its own planet. It grew out at me. It's going down the halls now. It's growing this way. And it—"

"Don't run away," came the voice over the intercom. This time it was the Kenneth voice.

"You see," Sibyl said, "it *calls* to me. Like Kenneth calling to me in my Radix dream. But this time he's there, somewhere. And suppose I go to it. Or suppose I don't go to it. You see—" and Sibyl broke off a high, hysterical giggle.

"Don't get hys—"

"Sibyl!" came the call over the intercom.

"Hysterical. I loathe trying to cope with hysterical women. We'd best get to the control room before it does." Dr. Beadle picked up his black bag.

"Oh, yes. Yes. I think it could... yes, it could take over the whole ship. Open doors. Go everywhere. Turn on lights...."

Sibyl swallowed, trembling not with fear now, but with the effort of staying calm. The terrible necessity of facing another crisis when she was so tired, so weak, so much needing someone to let her rest, to take care of her.

She edged the cabin door open cautiously, drew a sharp breath. Brilliant lights streamed down the hall. The Radix plant had been turning on lights as it came. Naturally, Stuart knew where everything was. It was feeding itself with light. Keeping itself awake with light.

"Hurry," she said, because she could see the green reaching at the top of the gangway now and they'd have to go right past it.

"And you said we could control it," Dr. Beadle said. "It's only a plant, you said. And now you're scared to death."

"No, I'm not. It *is* only a plant." Sibyl slowed as they reached where it was growing. "You can stand here inches away from where it's growing and it can't hurt you."

And then she screamed. Because bumping up the steps was a growth like a head. Like Kenneth's head — caricatured and distorted — and its mouth moved and it called, "Sibyl! Help me!"

Dr. Beadle grabbed for her arm but it was too late. She was running toward the Radix plant. And she tripped on a vine at the top of the stairs and fell halfway down. As she moved to get up, painfully finding she'd sprained an ankle, she looked up to see a purple flower looming over her head.

"Kenneth!" she called.

"Welcome to Radix," the Stuart voice said.

Sibyl reached back and pulled off the flower. But there were flowers growing at her all over, now. At her chin, her legs, her arms. She could feel them sticking at her with some slimy ooze, and as she brushed them off, pulled at them, more came at her.

"I'm sorry," Dr. Beadle called. "But I've got to get to the control room before it's too late."

"But it's *got* me. It'll — no it won't," she realized suddenly. Or it would have already. She was immune to the virus types Radix had manufactured for use on Centaurians and humans. So until it manufactured another it was helpless.

Not quite. As she wrested the vines from herself, one of the butterfly plants came slowly floating up the stairs and wrapped her head and her mouth. As Sibyl clawed it away so she could breathe, another one settled over her head, and then she felt a ropelike stem twisting around her neck, while more of them grew about her feet, pressing into her swollen ankle painfully.

She screamed for Dr. Beadle, but he was long gone, now. She clawed and bit at the vine, until she had bitten her own lips bloody, and now she was suffocating and suddenly— All the lights went off. For a moment Sibyl thought she'd gone blind and then she realized Dr. Beadle had done that from the control room. Just in time. The vine stopped growing. She pulled the gauzy butterfly plant from her face, clawed and bit at the vines that held her until she was loose, and then, on her hands and knees, felt her way to the control room.

She knocked on the door, called, and Dr. Beadle let her in. The room was eerie with only the little light from the dials.

"I thought you had deserted me," she said, dragging herself all the way into the room and closing the door behind her. "I never thought I'd be so glad to see you."

"There's no reason to be sentimental," Dr. Beadle said. "I did desert you. But after I got in here I thought of turning off the lights, as we did when we communicated with Stuart for navigational instructions. Are you really unable to walk or are you just showing off?"

"It's easier this way. I believe I've sprained my ankle and having it half crushed by a vine didn't help it any."

"Here. Sit on the bunk and I'll tape it for you. That was an idiotic thing you did and it endangered me and the ship. You don't seem to have fractured a bone. Does that hurt?"

"Hell, yes, it hurts. You wouldn't understand why I ran for that thing that looked like Kenneth, so I won't try to explain it. But Kenneth did tell me before to destroy all of the Radix plant."

"Obviously. We can't even get to the galley to get something to eat. But it'll take a long time for it to die in the dark, and I haven't even had breakfast."

Sibyl's ankle hurt badly and it was so hard to think. What would kill a plant quickly? Freezing. "We could turn the thermostat to zero. About five hours ought to kill it off good. Then we can dump it into space and turn the lights back on."

Sibyl limped over to the thermostat, turned it down, got a couple of blankets off the bunk and handed one to Dr. Beadle.

"You can sleep first," he said. "And if you'll chew up this pill — no, that one's the cyanide, it's the orange one — it'll kill the pain in your ankle."

"I'm not sleepy," Sibyl said. "I've gotten a second wind and I'd never get to sleep. Besides, I've just had a wonderful idea." She got the brandy out from under the instrument panel. "Look! Almost a whole quart. And just you to share it with."

"I don't drink. If I get very cold I'll take a medicinal dose of it."

"Well, *I* drink. I'll drink for both of us and I'll drink to you and me, because there isn't anybody else."

Four hours later Sibyl was still drunk. She felt marvelous and everything that had ever happened to her seemed wonderful and funny.

"Beadsy," she said, leaning fondly against him, "I wish I liked you. You're the only man around for millions of miles."

"I have no desire for you to like me," Dr. Beadle answered stiffly. He moved away a little. "I'm not that cold."

"Oh, but you *are*," Sibyl sighed. "That's just what you are. Unbearably cold. I'll bet your mother used to prop your bottle. Did she prop it, Beadsy?"

"My first name is Wilfred."

"How awful for you. Still, it's no excuse. You could have called yourself Fred. Tell me why, out of all the millions of men in the world, I have to spend weeks alone in a spaceship with *you*! Why aren't you a nice, dirty old man? A nice, warm, dirty old man?"

Dr. Beadle withdrew further into his blanket, held up the luminous dial of his watch to see there were forty-five minutes left before the five hours were up. "You are unable to carry on a reasonable conversation," he said. "We will therefore not converse."

Sibyl felt for the main light switch, threw it on, and blinked her eyes in the sudden light. Somehow, it sobered her and made her feel the cold. It was bitter cold. Cold as death and eternity.

"Well," she said. "Here goes the moment of truth." She pushed the door aside. Something crackled and broke on the other side. Sibyl looked out into a sparkling, frosted fairyland. The Radix plants had frozen into beauty, and here and there green fountains of frozen sap hung motionless in the cold.

She ducked her head into the control room. "It's all over but the machete work," she said. "Rollo."

"That's better than Beadsy," Dr. Beadle said. He came over, still draped in his blanket and looked down the glittering hall. "We'd best dispose of all this before we defrost. Otherwise we'll leave a mess on the floor."

Sibyl sighed, trying to ignore her aching ankle, and pushed the last of the frozen, crackling plants into the disposal unit. It had been slow work, because there was so much of it, and it had to be broken to go into the unit. Dr. Beadle made all the trips and Sibyl did all the pushing. They cleared everything out of the hydroponics room, including every ounce of vermiculite and all the troughs.

"And now we spray," Sibyl sighed with a tired sigh, "after I have another cup of that broth. We spray with a bio-poison and shower and put our clothes through a sterile wash and then I'm going to sleep forever. You might as well sleep, too. If the ship does anything funny, there's not a thing either one of us can do about it."

"*You,*" said Dr. Beadle sarcastically, "can always get drunk."

CHAPTER X

There was the clank of metal on metal and Sibyl stood by the air lock, waiting for the navigator from Grant, Inc., to connect ships. She couldn't believe the moment. She'd prepared herself to die so many times — when she started out on the trip, when they reached Radix, when little Joe died, when the Radix plant erupted on the ship. And now all that was about to turn into a wild dream. Now they'd be safe.

She had an odd feeling of slight regret. As though this life she had fought so violently for was not going to be worth it after all.

But when the spruce young navigator stepped in and looked at her uncertainly, as though it might be an impertinence to smile at her after whatever vicissitudes she had just been through, Sibyl grinned.

"You," she said, "are the first man I've seen in two months."

"Then Dr. Beadle —"

"Oh, Beadsy's still here. Tell me. Do *you* drink?"

The young man cleared his throat and tried to stop looking surprised, "Not constantly," he said. And then smiled. He was a short, stocky man about thirty-five, with furry-looking black hair and small hazel eyes. "Name's Steerforth Cade, Sergeant Blue. Friends call me Steer."

"Drinking companions call me Sibyl. Steerforth's a good name for a navigator."

Steer removed his hat, turned it in his hands as he spoke. "After a character in Dickens. A bad sort. Seduced Little Em'ly."

"Well!" Sibyl said. "Things are looking better and —"

"Don't you think," Dr. Beadle said, coming in with a cough, "you'd better navigate the ship, Mr. Cade, before you and Mrs. Blue start all that?"

Steer winked at Sibyl and made for the navigation room with Dr. Beadle behind him to make sure he did what he was supposed to.

As for Sibyl, she went for her bath and make-up. She showered quickly, rouged her knees and took the only remaining wrap-around dress out of its cellophane. She pinned it into a low drape under her left shoulder, brushed her hair into its shiny stripes, pinched her eyebrows into tidier shape and gave herself a grin in the mirror.

"We've been through a lot together, me and me," she said softly to her image. "Don't give up just because we've won."

Sibyl made for the kitchen and got an omelet with freeze-dried mushrooms, green onions and a spot of white wine ready for the pan. It was the best she could do, with almost nothing left in the pantry. Oh, and a touch of garlic powder. Then she set a bowl of tomatoes to hydrate and opened a pack of rolls.

She found Steer and Dr. Beadle in the lounge.

"...the hormonal output of a woman her age," Dr. Beadle was saying. "If you simply ignore, as I did—"

"Ah," Sibyl said as she came in. "You're discussing your mother, Beadsy. I can tell. If she'd had the proper hormonal output she'd have nursed you, and that would have made all the difference, though I wouldn't want to hurt your feelings by saying so."

"That was *not*—" Dr. Beadle began, but Steer interrupted.

"Discussing fuel additives," Steer said, standing up to take Sibyl's hand and settle her on the sofa. "Dr. Beadle seems to be an inactive sort of expert. And speaking of fuel additives, where are the storage tanks around here?"

"Under the plant stand," Sibyl said. "We threw out the plants. I developed a strange aversion to potted plants. Gin and 'gin for me."

Dr, Beadle sat forward on the edge of his chair. "Mr. Cade, we have been out of touch with civilization for months. Tell me—how is National Lead doing?"

Steer laughed. "Don't know," he said. "Only bond I have is for my navigator's license. What'll it be for you?"

"Nothing. Then at least you've heard how Centaurian Imports are doing?"

"Up," Steer said, clicking the gin nozzle and then the 'gin. "Benzale murders have stopped and a Centaurian drug company found a herb on the Outer Islands that cures baldness by local application. Take me for a good example. Oh, and they found something else on the Outer Islands. You'll never guess what."

Dr. Beadle made a face. "Why guess? Why not just tell us?"

"An heir to Stuart Grant's estate. A son. He had none by his legal wife. But this... female... the mother, claims Stuart Grant spent a year on her island. And there's some big mystery about the son. The mother does all the talking — in broken Centaurian and English which she claims Mr. Grant taught her."

"Impossible," Dr. Beadle said. "Stuart Grant spent his life on Earth, except for brief trips to Centaurus."

A memory flickered on in Sibyl's mind. "No. It was kept secret, but he ran away to Centaurus when he was sixteen. But Centaurians and Terrans are mutually sterile."

"Civilized Centaurians," Steer said. "This female Centaurian is an offshoot race, isolated thousands of years from the mainland Centaurians, and subject to constant radiation from a uranium deposit nearby in the sea. Must be an odd-looking bunch, by and large."

"Nonsense!" Dr. Beadle said. "Mrs. Blue, are you preparing dinner or are you just going to sit there and drink?"

"Both," said Sibyl, frowning to herself at the thought of Stuart's having a son. Somehow the thought made her uncomfortable, as though he weren't gone, after all. "Is the female humanoid?"

Steer whistled. "Is she ever! If you don't mind a few blond scales. The Hammond papers had color slicks of her the day I left."

"And... the son?"

"That's part of the mystery. She's gotten him hidden away somewhere. Nobody knows if he's on Centaurus or Earth, or why he's hidden."

"I'm hungry," Dr. Beadle interrupted. "And I'm *not* interested in the conversation. All I want to do is get back to Earth as quickly and safely as possible and I'd certainly appreciate it if Mr. Cade would concentrate on that."

Sibyl finished off her drink and said, "Oh, all right," and went to the kitchen. She warmed the omelet pan and gave the eggs another stir, but her mind was full of images of what Stuart's child by a humanoid Centaurian would look like. And she couldn't put from her mind the Stuart-Radix plant she'd tended so long on the trip.

The child, she figured, if born during Stuart's visit at seventeen would now be... twenty-three years old. Good Lord! No child, that. Why had the mother kept quiet so long? Perhaps until the Centaurians came from the chemical company she heard nothing from the outside world. But how come a man of twenty-three didn't come forward to speak for himself?

Sibyl turned the omelet carefully, pulled out the rolls and sprinkled the hydrated tomatoes with vinegar and a few spices.

She buzzed for the men, and Steer, at least, appreciated the omelet.

After dinner Steer checked the instruments again, with Sibyl looking over his shoulder and telling him what agony she'd gone through with each of those little levers and buttons that he pressed with such facility.

"Well," Steer said, when they were back in the lounge with coffee and brandy, "what old spacemen discuss this close to home is, what's the first thing you want to do when we make Earthfall?"

"Me?" Sibyl said, taking a deep breath. "I want to smoke a cigar. A beautiful, golden Hellenic."

Steer laughed "Never saw anything in smoking, myself. Tried it a couple of times, didn't like. What I usually want to do is date up a pretty girl. How about it?"

"Sure," Sibyl said, "but we might as well get acquainted now. I gather you're not married. What's your life been like, anyhow? Unless you don't like to say."

"Married a long time," Steer corrected. He was quiet a moment, reaching for his coffee, and Sibyl had a chance to appraise his looks—heavy, black brows and that furry hair gave him an animal look that Sibyl enjoyed. And there was something animal about his slow speech, leaving out so often the beginning of sentences. And yet, obviously there was a quick intelligence all this masked. It made him fun to explore.

"Away a lot," Steer said finally. "Got five kids, three of them mine. I like it that way. She likes it that way. Perfect marriage. Great girl. What do you think?"

"Fine," Sibyl said. And thought how she'd have hated it if it had had to be that way with Kenneth, but it hadn't. "Only most people aren't that sensible. Let's drink to your wife. And the memory of my husband and the general incredibility of life."

"Yep," Steer said agreeably, and clicked glasses and drank and then smiled. "My life's pretty ordinary, though. But come to think of it, maybe it isn't, flying to another star system all the time. But that's all I do — drive there and drive back. Taxi driver."

Sibyl watched his heavy, hairy wrist as he poured and hoped he wouldn't be fat, dull and retired in ten years. Sometimes they did that, and Steer would run to fat. But his wife wouldn't let that happen. She sounded too interesting to let him go to pot.

Sibyl leaned back against the strong shoulder Steer presented to her and sighed happily. "I like you," she said. "And I like your wife and your children. And there's something about your work you regret. What was it you really wanted?"

Steer grinned down at her face and kissed her softly. His mouth was large and warm and somehow... Earth-normal. "There *was* something, you perspicacious little minion of the law. But just now I forget what it was." He kissed her again, closer this time.

"Come on," Sibyl said, getting up. "Bring your gear on into the captain's cabin. It's bigger. And it's got a better bed."

Dr. Beadle stood by the view port, watching the Earth circle under the ship, pointing out the continents and growing unusually loquacious over Africa and the origin of sickle-cell anemia.

Steer was busy now, and Sibyl smiled, watching his sure way with the ship, his communications with Earth stations as they circled, the professional set of his shoulders.

She hadn't fallen in love with Steer the way she had with Stuart. But she liked him fondly and felt a pride in him and hoped he'd remember the date two weeks from now when he'd be back for his next run to Centaurus.

Earth got closer. Sibyl began to wonder if Stuart Grant's son were there somewhere, or on Centaurus, and if she'd ever get to see him, or even his picture. Would he look like Stuart at all? And what would she feel if he did? Maybe Scaley Moe would know something. It would be good to see Scaley Moe again.

And then she thought how she was going to see Missy again and such an excitement filled her she bit her lip to keep from laughing with joy. Would she have grown in any way? Changed? Had any trouble come her way with Sibyl not there? Oh, Missy...

"Well," Sibyl said to Dr. Beadle when the ramp was going down, "I guess we won't see each other any more."

"I guess not," Dr. Beadle said impatiently. "And don't forget that a woman your age should go through the Schenthal computer twice a year. Please go ahead. I want to get to a newspaper and see where National Lead is today."

Sibyl laughed and went down the ramp and Missy was there. Straight and tall and looking mature with a new hairdo. But still so much the same Missy she'd been at the age of three, that tears streamed out of Sibyl's eyes and all she could say was, "Missy! Missy!"

Steer came by and squeezed her arm and smiled at her and Missy. "Bye," he said. "Until the twelfth."

"Oh, this is my daughter," Sibyl said.

"Can tell that. Good to know you, Missy. See you in a fortnight."

"Who's that?" Missy asked as they walked to a limousine waiting at the edge of the landing strip.

"My latest boy friend. Isn't he cute?"

The limousine drove on smoothly, through the familiar streets, home.

"He looks a little young to be my father," Missy was saying. "But I do so want you to marry somebody who'll keep you home. Auntie was nice, but I *missed* you so much."

"Missy, I'll never marry again. I'm even surer of it now than I was before the trip. Have you saved the newspaper accounts about Stuart's supposed son?"

Missy looked startled. "Something with you and Mr. Grant?"

The limousine stopped behind their apartment house. "No," Sibyl laughed. "I got over him long before he... died. I'm wondering if this is going to be a case for me. I mean, I know it's a federal case, but if the boy might by any chance be hidden in Hammond— Hey! What do you think you're doing?" Sibyl yelled to a reporter with a camera as she stepped out of the car.

"They were supposed to be kept away," Missy said.

"On the spot!" The newsman grinned nastily.

Sibyl was on him in one leap. She rammed her shoulder into his stomach and ripped the wire from the sound recorder with her hand at the same time. The camera hit the ground with a crash and the man's head landed on one comer of it.

He rolled over, cursing, and came at Sibyl with murder in his eyes. Sibyl, unruffled, dodged the left to her chin and watched him dent his fist on the side of the limousine.

"Amateur!" she called, and let the door to the building close behind her just as he got to it. She locked it from the inside, just to be sure, and took the escalator up with Missy.

"Well!" Missy said admiringly. "That's the first time I've seen my dear old gray-haired mom at work. Not bad! But about Stuart Grant's son — before we were so rudely interrupted — There's another one lurking in the hall!"

Sibyl had one high-heeled shoe off as they came around the corner, and almost brought it down on a brunette boy's head before she saw who it was.

"Jimmy!" she gasped.

Stanley Rauch, who was patrolling her door, came up before Jimmy could open his mouth. "This boy here insisted he was a friend of the family, and I remember him from the Gracia Joad case — how he helped — so I... I hope it's all right."

Sibyl shook Stanley's hand hard and then turned to Jimmy.

"I just thought," Jimmy said, "that you and Missy might need some protection. I've been sort of looking after Missy since you left. Reporters came around after you left and all, and her aunt's husband was out of town a lot and..." his voice trailed off as his earnest look went from Sibyl to Missy.

The earnest look changed to one of sheer idiocy. Missy returned it by examining the tips of her toeless shoes with rapt attention.

Sibyl smiled happily. Jimmy made a nice boy friend.

"Thank you," Sibyl told him. "Come back tomorrow. Right now I want to talk to Missy about something."

Missy pressed her key against the door. "I aired it out yesterday."

The apartment looked wonderful. Home. Missy had put a vase of yellow roses on the coffee table. And cigars and a gin and 'gin glass all ready.

"I'll get your gin and 'gin," Missy said. "They're all mixed in the fridge. And there's the afternoon paper from yesterday. The rumor now, as I was going to say, was that Stuart Grant's son is here in Hammond."

Sibyl picked up the vase of yellow roses and sank her nose into them. Always they reminded her of Kenneth. She'd worn yellow roses when they got married. Yellow —

Sibyl screamed and dropped the vase. It shattered and spilled across the floor and she screamed again.

It was Stuart Grant walking out of her bedroom. Missy ran in, and Stanley began pounding on the front door.

Sibyl found tears streaming down her face and great sobs of hysteria rose in her throat. Missy was holding her and saying to the apparition, "What are *you*?"

Green traceries ran down the man's throat and on his head was a silver, not a purple growth, that was perhaps raised scales. But it was so like... Sibyl got herself under control as quickly as she could.

"Nothing, Stanley," she said, opening the door hole. "Just female weakness. The excitement of coming home. You can go along now. I've got the door locked from the inside."

"Sure?" he asked anxiously.

"Absolutely," Sibyl said, but clung still to Missy and felt herself shaking all over. "I'll see you down at the station tomorrow. And maybe we can sneak out for a drink if I promise not to seduce you."

Stanley laughed and they heard his retreating footfalls.

The Stuart Grant apparition was sitting on the sofa examining one of Sibyl's cigars with great interest. It looked up and spoke, somehow wetly and with great hesitation over the words. "I am Dardl. You... were with... my progenitor?"

"Yes," Sibyl said. "Missy, this is Stuart Grant's son. Now get me that gin and 'gin."

The telephone buzzed. "Glad you're back, Sergeant Blue," said Lieutenant Brandt. "Frankly, I didn't doubt for a minute you'd come through. Everybody here sends love. But all that can wait. Come on down to headquarters. I've got an assignment for you."

Sibyl laughed. "Now I know I'm home. Don't I even get time to take a bath and pretty up?"

Brandt made a noise. "Look. It's the Stuart Grant pretender to the throne. His mother says he's been kidnapped. And I think we ought to have you right on it, because you've just done the Stuart Grant case and on account of your Centaurian contacts."

"Give my love to everybody and I'll be down when I can. Although how I'm going to do anything with those Centaurian charges against me hanging fire, I don't know."

"The charges were dropped long ago. You're as pure as a newborn babe."

"Ha!" Sibyl said, and clicked off.

Dardl was eating the cigar and Sibyl snatched it out of his mouth.

"That's a twenty-five cent Hellenic," she said. "What did you come to me for, Dardl Grant?"

"If you know that I am my progenitor's progeny." He looked away in embarrassment when he saw that what Sibyl did with the cigar was light it.

Sibyl looked at those eyes—the shape of them though they were lashless—that nose and mouth, the set of the shoulders. For a moment the helpless pain of love, the familiar knot of emotion came back to her. All that she had felt for Stuart filled her. And then it went away.

"Yes," Sibyl said. "You are."

He sighed—a sort of bubbling sound. "You were... his friend."

"Yes." Was the man mentally defective, or was it his struggle with the language? Something about him...

"Then," said Dardl, "I believe you his only friend. Mother found no others. So I come to you. To know."

Sibyl took the gin and 'gin from Missy, and found herself badly startled. Stuart's only friend. She had loved Stuart, hated Stuart. But never felt sorry for him. Was he to haunt her now?

"How did you get here?" Sibyl asked.

He grinned, revealing a set of pointed teeth. "A Centaurian—Llanr—brought me. We hiding in his small room. I ask Llanr. He brought me last night in the dark."

138

Scaley Moe! She thought of all the cases he'd helped her with, one way or another. And Brandt had once wanted her to pin something on him and run him in!

"So I could tell you I'm sure Stuart Grant was your father?"

"Also," said Dardl, "I want to return to my beloved island and the salt sea." To Sibyl's surprise he burst into tears. "Oh, I am so alonely."

Missy went over and sat by him, taking his hand in an instinctive maternal gesture. "How old are you?" she asked.

He sobbed a moment. "Only six," he said, and held up a flabby bit of leathery material he wore on a string around his neck. "My egg," he said. "Of all my brothers, me she picked to bring. They play on the sands and here I am so alonely."

"Six!" Missy said. "That must be by some Centaurian reckoning. Are you a child?"

"A youngling," he said. "Me and the others."

Sibyl was frowning to herself as the import of "the others" sank in on her. "How many others?"

"Eleven."

"All exactly like you?"

He nodded. "The same hatching, and our mother lent us out for nursing. She watched so that none of us were eaten by the Carder. We are the only batch on the island with so many that lived," Dardl finished up proudly.

"Whew!" Sibyl said, and downed the rest of her drink.

"But I want to go home. You are my father's friend and you must help my mother to understand."

"I will," Sibyl said, "but right now I'm going to call Llanr to take you back to his house and I'll see about all this later. Missy, dial Scaley Moe at three six-nine nine-four eight-eight."

Sibyl stumped out her cigar and said, "Hi," when Scaley Moe came on.

"Ah," he said. "My soft, white gleerl blossom. So you have returned. And when can I —"

"Right now," Sibyl said. "You must come take this child home. If you bring a hat and he keeps his head down I think you can get him to the car all right."

"But you will not desert him, will you, my kindhearted friend?"

"Of course not. Only I wonder what you've got up your sleeve."

"Sleeve? Nothing."

"Missy," Sibyl said when Scaley Moe left with Dardl, who insisted on embracing her ecstatically on departure, "we answer no doorbells and no telephone, even if it's Brandt, and I am going to eat and have a monumental, wallowing bath and sleep forever."

"I've got steaks," Missy said.

After dinner Sibyl bathed in Float Foam and drank three more gin and 'gins and put on her prettiest beige negligee and a lot of make-up and then didn't feel like sleeping after all. So she got out her map of Plataea — the conjectural sites of the fifth century B.C. — opened Thucydides, Book II, where she'd left off, and began reading.

Missy walked in and giggled.

"What's the matter?" Sibyl asked, looking up from the depths of an irregular aorist participle.

"Nothing. Most people don't dress up like that to read Greek, that's all."

"For six months I've worn nothing but ugly plastic wrap-around dresses. Anyway, I think Thucydides is snappy enough to dress up for. Night."

"Night."

Sibyl awakened from a luxurious sleep the next morning to the braying of the telephone.

"Yes?"

"Brandt here," the answering voice said impatiently. "Junior came back so I left you alone yesterday evening. But now we know where the heir is and Scaley Moe is going to get the mother a good lawyer and if the Schenthal computer has a gene typing on Stuart Grant — and no doubt it does — there shouldn't be any problem about establishing paternity. Naturally Scaley Moe is going to take a good, fat fee from Dardl's claim."

"Why not?"

"And besides, we're going to have to keep an eye on Scaley Moe. The island females on Garlg — where Dardl's from — are much more humanoid than mainland Centaurian females. That is, they make human women look castrated. Now that Scaley Moe knows this, I'll bet my bottom dollar he's going to try to import—"

"I haven't had my morning coffee yet," Sibyl said. "I'm sitting here shaky and starving in my beautiful beige nightie. See you later."

Sibyl switched off, stretched happily and looked up to see Missy coming in with a cup of coffee. "Ah, Hebe with my nectar. What day is it?"

"Tuesday. I've got school, unless you think you might need me."

"Nope. Got a busy day ahead. I want to see Joe Rabinsky's widow and check in with Brandt and maybe see what I can do about poor Dardl." Sibyl wondered briefly about comforting Stuart's widow, and then decided it wouldn't be exactly appropriate.

Sibyl had Joe's wallet in her purse and she tried to remember the things he had said, but all she could think of was his big, hurt eyes. She took the sidewalks to the poorer section of Hammond, near Old Town, went into the shoddy building of tight little ugly apartments and found 3A.

A very pregnant young woman answered the door, eyed Sibyl suspiciously, and then showed a shy smile and said, "You're Mrs. Blue. I saw on television. How come you knew about me?"

"Joe told me. I've brought you his wallet and... his love."

The girl burst into tears. "To think he remembered! He told me he wasn't going to that planet, and then when he went anyway, I thought he was giving me a line. And maybe the wedding ceremony was a fake or something."

Sibyl said firmly, "It wasn't a fake and I'll check it for you just so you'll be sure. Are you all right about money?"

"Right now. I worked for a while but now I can't work no more. I don't know what after the baby. And to think Joe really cared about me! He said so to you?"

Sibyl told Mrs. Rabinsky everything she remembered that Joe had ever said, and added a few improvisations about the baby. Then she went quickly through Joe's papers with her, found a fairly substantial insurance policy and promised to see about Joe's back wages from Grant, Inc.

And left with a promise to be the baby's godmother. Somehow it hadn't been sad, as she'd thought it would be.

The girl was so happy that Joe had really cared about her. And Sibyl found herself looking forward to being a godmother and holding the baby in her arms and going to see it now and then and taking it to the zoo when it got older.

It was three days later that Brandt pulled her next assignment on her. "Well," he said, "you're lucky. It's a vacation, actually."

Sibyl frowned. "I can tell by the saccharine expression on your face that it's going to be something I don't like."

"But you *will* like it. The only trouble is that it involves a little trip and you may not feel like traveling again just yet."

"I certainly don't," Sibyl said emphatically. She folded her arms over her chest and prepared to hold out forever.

Brandt cleared his throat. "Actually, it sort of winds up the Stuart Grant case. And the State Department insists. It seems you're the only person on Earth that Dardl really trusts. And you speak Centaurian and you're clever and dependable."

"Now listen," Sibyl said. "You seem to forget I'm a family girl. And I promised not to leave Missy again until she gets to college, which is a year off."

"Nobody said you had to leave Missy. The State Department is offering to pay you to chaperon Dardl back to his idyllic little island and to get to know him and his brothers. You and Missy could go together and stay a couple of months and get back in time for the fall term. It would be a terrific experience for her."

Sibyl unfolded her arms. It might be fun, at that "What's wrong with Dardl's mother?"

"Didn't I warn you about Scaley Moe? She's decided she likes it here, and her maternal instincts ran out some time ago. The children are supposed to fend for themselves from the time they're two — Centaurian reckoning — and Dardl's six. But the State Department's very interested in keeping Dardl and his brothers happy — for interplanetary reasons. They're going to be pretty powerful in a few years, with a half-interest in Grant, Incorporated. They'll need to be educated and everything, but first they need an initial sort of explanation about what civilization is. And the State Department and Grant, Incorporated, both want a discreet report about the brothers, so they'll know what they're going to have to contend with."

Sibyl thought a moment. Maybe Missy *would* enjoy a trip like that. And living on that island, away from civilization for a couple of months — that sounded nice. And poor Dardl. Sibyl didn't like to think of entrusting him to anyone else. Missy had shown a natural tenderness for him and his childishness. She'd be good with them.

Then Sibyl remembered Steer. If they left on the twelfth, Steer would be the navigator, and *that* would certainly add something to the two-week trip to Centaurus.

"I'll ask Missy," Sibyl said finally.

Sibyl waved Jimmy and Missy out of the door for their last date before the Centaurus trip. Jimmy had grown up a lot. He'd lost his baby deer stare and his shoulders had squared, somehow, and when she looked at him she almost regretted her age.

But not quite. She lit a delicate, golden cigar and got herself a gin and 'gin. "If you could see Missy now, Kenneth," she whispered softly to herself, and then glanced at the clock, downed the rest of the drink, had a quick shower, made a split-second decision on beige underwear and pulled on a slinky beige satin dress.

Gold jewelry and very pink make-up.

She looked pretty good when she was finished. I'm lucky, she thought. Here I've got a beautiful daughter, a good figure no matter how much I eat, naturally curly hair.

Even, she smiled at herself in the glass as the doorbell sounded, a man.

"Ready?" Steer asked.

"I'm always ready," Sibyl said.

The lifeblood of every author is audience feedback. Please consider leaving a review (of whatever length) on Amazon, GoodReads, or your favorite platform.

About the Author

Hugo Finalist **Rosel George Brown** exploded onto the science fiction scene in 1958, regularly appearing in *The Magazine of Fantasy and Science Fiction, Amazing Stories, Fantastic Universe,* and elsewhere. Two of her best stories were published in our *Rediscovery: Science Fiction by Women (1958-1963)*.

Her hit 1966 novel, *Sibyl Sue Blue,* a.k.a. *Galactic Sibyl Sue Blue,* poised her at the edge of superstardom. Sadly, her life was cut short by lymphoma in 1967, snuffing out one of the brightest lights of science fiction's Silver Age. It has been our pleasure to "rediscover" this lost luminary, bringing her work to life for a modern audience.

About the Publisher

Founded in 2019 by Galactic Journey's Gideon Marcus, **Journey Press** publishes the best science fiction, current and classic, with an emphasis on the unusual and the diverse. We also partner with other small presses to offer exciting titles we know you'll like!

Also available from Journey Press:

Rediscovery: Science Fiction by Women (1958-1963)

Kitra - Gideon Marcus   **I Want the Stars** - Tom Purdom